STR8 UP

Written by
CHUCK CONRAD

Table of Contents

THE HUSTLE

The gym is hot, the sound of cheers and boos mixed in bring excitement to Aiden's mind. *"I love this shit."* He thinks to himself, *"I was built for this."* He dribbles the ball in the middle of the court near the top of the 3 point line, just as his father taught him. He could see a group of elder men looking with focused eyes. The old players from the neighborhood that everybody knew ran shit on the low. The type of men most of your friends' mothers had some type of dealing with in the past. The type your father may have worked for before or was afraid of. One elder man in particular, Brock, better known in the streets as Whiskey, gave Aiden a head nod, indicating the unspoken message of handle your business. The time in the game is running out and his team is down by one. Aiden knows he's going to win the game. He has visualized himself winning this game before the game even started. He hears his best friend, Yogi, his ride or die yelling, "Send these niggas home mad, bro, the young thots are waiting." He laughed to himself and smiled at Yogi. He wipes the sweat from this thick brow, checks the time clock one last time, 8 seconds left, and looks his defender in the eye, *"This bum ass Nigga can't guard me"* he mumbles to himself. The defender vaguely hears the mumble and slaps the floor and presses Aiden with tough physical defense. Aiden is strong and quick. He easily blows past the defender with a left to right cross over driving to the right side of the court, he used a little of his left elbow to ensure the defender stays behind him, as the other team's next defender try to step up for help defense, Aiden spins away from the defender to the left almost causing the defender behind him and the help defender to crash into each other. Aiden found himself in the paint near the free throw line, his sweet spot, he can hear his father's voice in his head "get to your sweet spot, keep the game simple." He pulled up for a jump shot and holds his follow through as he looks at the ball go through the rim as time expires. "Get the fuck outta my Gym," he yells as his teammates rush him in celebration. He closes his eyes and listens for his favorite sound in basketball. "Fuck man," "where was the help," "I did help" "Play better fucking D next time muthafucka." "Fuck you" "Fuck you with your bitch ass." Yes, those were the sounds Aiden loved to hear. He knew he played well if the opposite team was arguing and fighting each other. He considers it a lost if he didn't hear that after games.

The sound of Yogi's voice broke Aiden's victory mediation. Yogi was super excited singing O.T. Genasis song "I be getting to the money, everybody mad." Aiden joined in the singing laughing with his best friend. "I be getting to the money." Whiskey signaled for Aiden and pointed towards the bathroom. Aiden told Yogi he would be right back and Yogi followed him, stopping a few feet from the bathroom doors. Yogi was protective of Aiden that way. Yogi loved Aiden he was the only person in the world that made him feel special, that included him and made him feel loved and like they were family. Yogi told himself he would die for Aiden, his brother. Aiden walked into the bathroom where Whiskey and several other elder men were.

One white elder man with khakis pants and white short-sleeve-button down shirt, and a non-lit cigar in his hand was fussing at the Hispanic defender and the coach of the other team, "What the fuck is wrong with y'all, y'all know he's not going to pass the ball, double his ass and make someone else beat us." The Hispanic kid and Aiden locked eyes for a brief second and Aiden gave him a head nod and a smirk and the Hispanic kid smacked his lips said, "Yeah, alright."

Aiden and Whiskey shared a laugh as the fussing elder man handed Whiskey an envelope. Whiskey was a tall, dark skinned tone man with deep brown eyes, hence the nickname, who dressed like he was 25 years old. He wore slim fitting jeans with rips in, with either white or black Balenciaga's gym shoes, and a form fitting polo, he talked in a smooth voice that made him seem unfazed and unbothered about things happening around him. His laid back demeanor only changed when he laughed so it made people unsure when he was upset or just regular. People believed it was just better to keep him laughing so you knew for sure he wasn't upset with you. Whiskey counted 5 thousand dollars from the envelope and handed it to Aiden. The Hispanic kid saw the transaction and shook his head in frustration. Aiden gave Whiskey a handshake and a man hug which is more of a shoulder bump and a pat on the back, Whiskey told him he played well and he can't wait until the next game because "We're going to get rich taking these old niggas money." The white elder interrupted, "Who the hell are you calling old?" And the elders erupted in laughter.

Aiden walked back to meet Yogi, who hadn't left the spot a few feet from the bathroom. Yogi was entertaining a few women and exchanging numbers with them. He wanted to text them the address for a victory party. Aiden smiled at Yogi being the ultimate setup man/party promoter/bodyguard. The three young ladies seemed entertained by Yogi and excited to see Aiden as he approached. "What y'all talking about?" "You muthafucka," Yogi said jokingly, "these ladies looking forward to hanging with us tonight. I told them we're going to have the smoke and the drinks so all they had to do was show up and leave their bougie at home tonight." Aiden looked at the three women and decided the chick with the hazel eyes was the one he wanted. "Yeah, today"s going to be a good day," he said to himself in his ice cube voice. Aiden smiled at the girl and she shyly smiled back at him but looked away eyebrows raised, like she heard somebody call her name. Aiden asked if they were coming tonight for sure, for reassurance. The super thick girl of the crew said, "Yeah, fo sho." Yogi responded with "Y'all better, we winners over here, we the real deal over here, you see who we running with, Whiskey our OG, and we're up next." The Thick young lady, was a beautiful bronze colored skin tone, she had a long ponytail hairstyle, soft make-up that highlighted her beauty and lip gloss that complimented her full lips.

She sarcastically asked Yogi, "Y'all fuck with Whiskey huh?" She then asked, "So what do you do for

Whiskey, it's clear what this tall handsome jock with his perfect fuck-boy hair line up does for him," pointing at Aiden "But what do you do?" touching Yogi's shoulder, Yogi feeling little and like she was testing his nuts at the moment said, "I'm the killa, I kill shit, that's what I do." He said this loudly with confidence as he was pounding his fist over his chest. Just as he was pounding his chest Whiskey and the elders walked by and Whiskey said, "Is that what you do for me, Yogi Bear?" he said smiling, "More like Aiden's cheerleader," said one elder, and Aiden put his hand over his eyes shaking his head no, embarrassed for his friend trying to hide his smile. The girls and the elders burst out in laughter as Yogi rocked back in forth with his hands in his pocket says, "Come on Whiskey, I'm more like his hype man, why I got to be a cheerleader." Whiskey laughed and said, "I like you, Yogi; I like you," and walked away giving a quick head nod to Aiden. Aiden looks back at the hazel-eyed young lady who was now looking at him. He smiled and reached out to shake her hand. He said," I'm Aiden," and she said," I'm Zari." The thick woman provided her number to Yogi and turned and walked away. Yogi no longer embarrassed, turned to Aiden and asked if he got paid. Aiden said, "Yeah, why?" Yogi then said, "I'm going to need five dollars because they Hot N' Ready." Referring to the little Caesar pizza chain they love to eat. They both laugh and begin walking out of the gym.

Zari and the other three ladies all talked about their encounter with Aiden and joked about how Yogi was a wannabe thug but super cool. The thick friend whose name is Carla said laughingly, "I'd give Yogi fat ass some pussy and have him bring me food, cuddling, and shit when I'm lonely and my niggas ain't acting right." The girls laughed and Carla asked Zari, "Are you going to let Aiden hit that?" "Shit, girl I would, I would ride that pretty ass face of his and then ride that dick, have him all in love and shit." Zari and the girls laughed but Zari

4

wasn't feeling it. Aiden wasn't her type but he was fine. Zari liked dark skin tone nerdy type dudes. She was more into the intellectual and philosopher-type guys. She watched her mom and sisters date dudes like Aiden and she wasn't feeling him like that but again, "*He is fine though*," she thought to herself. Staring at Zari, Carla said while laughing "Yeah, bitch you're going to let him fuck." All the girls joined in laughing now. Just as they were about to get in Zari's car, Zari felt someone pull her hand. She turned around and it was the Hispanic kid. "Zari, is that the type of niggas you fuck with?" Zari, now a little irritated, yelled, "Damn, Israel, what the fuck, bro?" Israel said, "I saw you talking to them buster ass dudes, you too good to fuck with that wannabe playboy and that little fucking clown sidekick." Zari and the girls laughed but Vera the third girl of the crew, said, "You're just mad y'all got y'all ass kicked again. Stop being a sore loser Israel." Israel then said aggressively, "Don't fuck with them, nothing good going to come from it." Zari said to Israel. "Nobody is thinking about them we trying to get to the money so relax." Israel smacked his lips and said, "Yeah, aight." and they parted ways.

AIDEN

Aiden is 6'5" tall, light skin tone; he likes to refer to himself as a caramel American. He has a slim muscular build like a track star, strong thighs, and calves to match his long arms with nice bi and triceps. He has a bald fade with waves at the top of his head, so you can bet his du-rag and brush is not too far from him. He is a trendy dresser, always trying to wear what's currently in style, so skinny jeans and form-fitting shirts are a must for him. He swears the Nike Jordan basketball shoes are the best thing that happened to basketball life ever. In particular, he loved the 11's, the greatest shoe ever made in his eyes. He recently took over a lease for a Mercedes Benz S550 from Whiskey; Whiskey took the car back from one of his many women. Aiden felt like life was moving in the right direction for him and Yogi now. He had been playing basketball all his life with Yogi in his backyard. He never knew how good he really was because he wasn't allowed to leave his neighborhood block and he wasn't allowed to play in school because his mother was a devout Seventh-day Adventist who didn't believe in competition. She felt it was of the devil and tempted people to become aggressive. She allowed Yogi over to the house because he was not threatening and was very respectful. Aiden's mother died when he was thirteen years old and he went to live with his father Ahmad. Ahmad was Muslim but didn't overly preach at Aiden about his belief. Ahmad wanted to show Aiden his way of living by his actions not with his words. He allowed Aiden to play basketball at the parks but stayed with his mother's teaching of not allowing Aiden of playing in schools. Aiden's father lived in the country, about an hour from the city that Yogi and Aiden grew up in. Aiden still hung out with Yogi every weekend so they can keep their bond. Aiden viewed Yogi as a brother, someone like himself.

Aiden was socially awkward in school. Never really speaking to anyone and staying in his own lane. He dressed nice, talked to Yogi and didn't really pay attention to anything else. Aiden met Whiskey during his senior year of high school. Whiskey was dropping off a few kids from the basketball team and noticed the tall athletic built kid. Whiskey shouted to Aiden, "Hey, my man, do you play any ball?" Aiden replied back nervously, "Yes, but I'm not allowed to play outside of my neighborhood park or backyard." Whiskey thought what the fuck and had a confused expression on his face and then laughed. He handed Aiden a card and told him to call him, "but only when you grow a set of balls and start making decisions for yourself like a man." Aiden said thank you and turned to Yogi and walked away. As soon as Aiden got to Yogi, Yogi said, "Dog, do you know who that is?" And answering his own question Yogi said, "That's Whiskey, he runs the whole east side of town and he can change our lives, bro. What did he say?" Aiden responded, "He told me to call him when I grow a pair of balls." Yogi burst out laughing and said, "I guess we ain't never going to get on then," he then asked Aiden jokingly if his balls had developed yet. Aiden laughed and push Yogi and they walked to the bus stop.

They bused to Yogi's house every day after school where Ahmad would pick Aiden up before making the hour drive home. Aiden enjoyed his rides home with his father, they would talk about life. They talked about basketball, they talked about his mother; they talked about money and how to manage it. They talked about women and what types to avoid and what types to keep around. They would talk about Allah and his teachings but also discuss the differences in his mother's beliefs compared to his own. Then they would have dinner and go out back for some one-on-one basketball play. Aiden would destroy his father but enjoyed the lessons learned in those one-on-one sessions. He learned so many little "old man tricks" to create space to get the shot you wanted. This night, Aiden laid in his bed thinking to himself, holding the all-black card with just the name Whiskey on it and phone number in white letters and numbers. He thought, *"I am a man, I been had balls."* Aiden considered what he was about to do. He knew his father wouldn't be happy about him dealing with the type of person that Whiskey is. Aiden put the card under his pillow and thought to himself that he will think about it overnight and make a decision to call Whiskey or not. He was curious as to why Whiskey asked him about basketball and wanted to know more. He rolled over, closed his eyes, and mumbled, "God lead me."

Aiden got to Yogi's house and they headed out to school. Yogi was his usual self, joking and excited that they were about to be grown and done with school. Aiden was thinking about that too and how he didn't want to go to college right away like his father said he should do. Aiden wanted to live a little first, see what the world had to offer. He felt sheltered and felt that he had missed out on so much. He was a senior and still a virgin, he has never been on a date. Never had a drink or smoked weed like so many of the other kids in school. He wanted to be his own man and change who he was. He said to Yogi, "You know we are lames, right?" Yogi looking confused, replied, "You might be lame, my G, but I'm hot shit. These hoes just haven't caught on yet because they slow, hell, I might need a cougar who understands my worth." And he laughed. Aiden didn't laugh; he remained in thought, serious about his assessment of himself and his brother. "I got to change that Yogi," Aiden said. "I want people to respect us. I want us to live and get the hot girls and drive the hot cars. I'm going to call Whiskey and see what's up." "About time you grew some balls," Yogi replied. Aiden said, "Shut the fuck up, you ain't got no balls either." Yogi, grabbing himself, replied, "I got huge fucking Balls." "Wait til you get load of me." he said in his tony Montana voice. Aiden stopped before enter the school, took out the card, and called Whiskey. Whiskey answered in his smooth voice, "Talk to me." "Hello, Mr. Whiskey my name is Aiden, you gave me your card yesterday at the school asking me if I play ball." "Oh yeah."

Whiskey said, "I see, you grew a pair overnight. Aiden, let's hook up so I can tell you what I got planned for you." Aiden got an address from Whiskey and skipped school and met with him.

Whiskey had a ball game planned and they played ball and Whiskey was impressed by Aiden's skills. Whiskey knew he had a secret weapon no one had seen this kid play and he was going to make some money with him. Whiskey proposition Aiden and told him, "If you play for me, I will pay you five thousand a game that we win." Aiden was blown away by the amount of money Whiskey was offering and asked nervously, "Is that all I have to do?" "Yup, that's it," said Whiskey. "Just win little homie. But if you ain't no winner I have to cut you off." Aiden was nervous, he was thinking it had to be more to it than that, but five thousand a game that he wins. Oh, yeah he was all the way down. Aiden called Yogi and told him what Whiskey offered and that they would need to come up with lies tell his father so he could stay with Yogi every weekend until he had enough money to get his own spot. "Cool, I'll be your manager, we are about to get all the money and we are about to come up. It's about to happen. You're the shit at ball, bro, make that shit happen." Yogi stated excitedly.

A month later Aiden met up with Whiskey for his first game, Yogi right by his side, The first game was nerve-racking for Aiden but he had a great game and his team won and his legend began. In Aiden's first game he finished with 36 points 8 rebounds 9 assists and 5 steals. After the game, he couldn't believe how the money felt in his hands. Five thousand dollars for an 18-year-old kid, he thought in disbelief. He was on high, he took Yogi shopping and they got new clothes and shoes. They went out to eat and he noticed that when the word got out that he was running with Whiskey and he was one of Whiskey's boys. People spoke to him more, He got head nods from dudes that never even looked at him. He got stares from girls that didn't know he was in their class. Aiden was enjoying the new attention and Yogi probably a little more than him. Aiden's father had warned him about shady characters to watch out for but to experience something and being told about something are two different things. The smiles alone from the once out of my league girls would have Aiden's soldier at full attention. Aiden would go on to win again the following week and decided right then and there, this was going to be his future for as long as he could play and then he would go to college. He had to break the news to his father. He was terrified to tell his father alone and asked if Yogi would go with him. "You're a whole pussy, bruh," Yogi said, shaking his tilted head in disbelief. Aiden just looked at Yogi without responding while rubbing his handing over his waves. "Alright, homie, I gotcha, I guess this is what a manager's job is," Yogi stated. "We're going tonight and get it over with," said Aiden.

Ahmad picked Aiden up as he usually does, Yogi hopped in the back seat. Stunned Ahmad asked Yogi where you think you going. Aiden responded to Ahmad's question, "Oh we got a special project to turn in for extra credit." Ahmad looked at Yogi reluctantly but put the car in gear and pulled off. The car ride was silent for about 30 minutes of the drive. Aiden broke the silence, thinking to himself *"I'm my own man, I have balls."* He mistakenly blurted out to his father, "I have balls." Yogi burst out in laughter and Ahmad responded "Well, I hope you do, son." Yogi laughed some more and shook his head while smirking, looking out of the side window. Ahmad, noticing that his son looked uneasy, asked, "Hey, what's up, what's on your mind?" Aiden slowly and in a low voice said, "Dad, I don't want to go to college." Ahmad in total disbelief asked calmly, "what are you going to do then. You're ready to get out there and provide for yourself. You must have a plan. Tell me what your plan is?" Aiden decided not to lie to his father. He told him he met a guy and he was going to play basketball for him for 5 thousand a game. Yogi now frozen in pure shock was quietly waiting for Ahmad to respond. Surprisingly to Aiden and Yogi, Ahmad showed support for his son and said, "Whatever you want to do is up to you. You have to live by this decision, however."

Ahmad then asked Aiden again, "So what's your plan?" Aiden didn't really have one; he just knew he wanted to experience things and then go to college later, so that's what he told his father. Ahmad was disappointed, it was all in his face and he rode the rest of the car route in silence.

This is the second season Aiden has played for Whiskey and life has changed since that car ride with Yogi and his father. He had a Mercedes; he had his own place and now had his pick of women. He was still super nervous when he would talk to or be alone with women. He fell in love with the women he would sleep with. He would joke with Yogi that all the women were his girlfriends. Yogi would agree and call him a sucker for love ass nigga. Things were going well for Aiden, he threw the best parties after his games, he was well known around the city now. Him and Yogi could get into clubs for 21 and up if they wanted. Everybody knew he was Whiskey's boy; Aiden hadn't lost a game in the two seasons he had been playing and had saved up 60 thousand dollars which he kept at his father's home. His father told him to do this so he wouldn't have to worry about some knucklehead robbing him or some fast little girl turning him out and spending all his money before he can make it. Aiden was riding high feeling like life was finally giving him his just due.

After leaving the game Yogi noticed that the Mexican kid had been a little extra salty about losing to Whiskey's team. He asked Aiden, "Why is my man so tight about losing to y'all? Everybody loses to y'all," he said confused. Aiden laughed at Yogi's confusion and said he must hate winners and smiled. Yogi went to give Aiden a fist pound and let the thought go. They rode back to Aiden's apartment listening to Jay Z's album titled 4:44. Yogi asked, "Aiden, oh, are you trying to get knowledge or something?" Aiden responded, "I'm trying to have balance before we get into some ratchet shit." Yogi responded, "My dude, cut this shit off and put on some Kodak black or 21 Savage so we can get hyped for the night that's about to

11

happen." Aiden pulled up to his apartment and people was already in his parking lot waiting for the party to jump off. Playing music loudly, smoking weed and sipping out of double white foam cups. Aiden loved this scene; he had become used to it and looked forward to it after his games. He then sees her, Zari with the eyes. He gave Zari a head nod, she was looking good to him with her slim thick shape. She had changed clothes from earlier and had a sundress on that hugged her shape and pick his interest even more. He wanted her bad, he wanted her for his girl, he was thinking as he looked at her rock to the beat of the music playing. He opened his apartment doors and people flooded in.

The party was lit as fuck, People dancing, drinking, and making out. Aiden saw Yogi in the corner talking to the thick girl, Carla, and by the way she was smiling and laughing, Yogi has him one. So Aiden looked for Zari. When he saw her, she was on her phone texting, biting the corner of her lip with a focused expression on her face. Aiden hadn't noticed how full her lips were. He was finding himself more attracted to her each time he seen her. He approached her and asked, "Excuse me, miss, can you help me find this curly hair beauty that watched me play basketball earlier?" She looked up from the phone, poking her bottom lip out, raising her eyebrows and said, "Fuck it, does she have freckles, Sir?" Aiden notice her light freckles and smiled and said, "Yeah, I just found out she does." They both smiled and begin talking most of the night. The rest of the night Aiden wouldn't leave Zari's sight. Zari was no longer the shy girl he had met at the game, she was engaging and flirty. Aiden was thinking that he wanted her to stay but not just for tonight but from now on. He wanted her to be his girl. Just a few years ago, Aiden was afraid to even stare at a girl, let alone talk to a girl like Zari. She's different he said to himself. And as they danced, he found himself lost in her eyes and he asked her if she would stay the night with him. She responds, "Oh, you think I'm a hoe?" He said jokingly, "Naw, I just hope you got hoe tendencies. But for real, I want you and I'm not talking about just tonight. I want you around as much as you can handle." She responded, "Oh yeah, is that what you want. You sure you can handle that?" Aiden smiled and said, "I've been waiting for you my whole life."

Carla and Yogi now being next to them talking chimed in, "Zari girl, he just wants some pussy." Yogi and Carla laughed. And Zari and Aiden smiled at each other. The party had calm down. Aiden told Yogi to kick everybody out. Yogi did so happily so he can be alone with Carla. Aiden asked Zari if she was staying, she looked at him while tilting her head to the side, the right side of her curly afro resting on her face. Her eyes looking up towards her forehead, like she was lost in thought, she bit her bottom lip while looking at Aiden and rolled her eyes " I guess so" while smiling. Aiden was super excited, he was about to lock down the girl of his dreams. Aiden had turned towards Yogi to see if he had caught his excitement but Yogi and Carla were gone. Aiden invited Zari to his room, closed and locked the door behind him.

Aiden had lost his sense of time; Zari had made him feel special like no other woman had. He hoped he was doing the same for her. Zari was putting her clothes on and texting on her phone. She noticed Aiden looking at her. She then said, "Yeah, I'm texting Carla to see if she got home or if she's still here and letting my sisters know I'm on my way home so they can look out for me." Aiden wishing Zari would just spend the night but too afraid to just ask. He texted Yogi saying, "She is the one; Zari is wifee from now on. Where are you, bro?" Yogi didn't respond and Aiden put his basketball shorts on. Zari asked to use his bathroom, Aiden said, "You don't have to ask. You should get used to being here. Zari shot a quick smile before using her fingers like a comb to place her hair behind her left ear and entering the bathroom. Aiden yelled, "There are towels in the cabinet behind the door." Zari took a towel from the cabinet and did a quick wash up in his sink. She was thinking to herself "got me in here doing a hoe bath." She finishes cleaning herself and looked in the mirror with a blank stare and said, "Damn girl."

When she exits the bathroom Aiden jokes while nodding his head up and down and smiling said, "Ah, see, you do have hoe tendencies." They laughed and Aiden asked Zari to let him walk her to her car. They got down the stairs and Aiden notices Yogi's car was in the parking lot still and thought he must be up there sleep. "Carla must have put his ass to sleep," he mumbled. He was thinking how he was going clown Yogi in the morning. Averting his attention back to Zari, he was walking slightly behind her looking at her ass shake when she walked. He was excited and still couldn't believe he just slept with her and how she made him feel. Zari got in her car and Aiden made small talk inviting her back over asking if she can come back so they could watch movies together and he would cook for her. Zari said sure and smiled. Aiden looked up, he thought he heard something. He then noticed a car he hadn't seen before in the lot. It gave him the chills and he told Zari, he better get back in to check on Yogi and he took one last look at the two guys in the car and briskly walked back up the stairs to his apartment.

He got to the apartment door feeling relieved to have made it back to his place, he grabs the door handle to enter and he felt the cold hard metal on the back of his head. "Open the door mothafucka," the gunman said. The voice sound familiar but Aiden can't put a face to it. Aiden was nervous and fear was starting to sink in. "Where is Yogi?" Aiden thought of Yogi as he entered the apartment with the gun to the back of his head, he attempted to throw his body into the gunman to get separation and to close the door but he stumbles over the bottom of the door entryway. He and the Gunman fall to the ground. The Gunman jumped back to his feet quickly and Aiden filled with fear crawled backwards, pulling himself with his right hand and holding his left hand up in the air pleading with the gunman. "Why the fuck are you doing this?" The Gunman ignoring the question

14

yelled, "Where the money at, huh?" Aiden then sees two more men enter his apartment and they start beating him, repeating "Where is the money?" "Where is the money?" Aiden is in complete shock and in total fear for his life. He's breathing hard and he has never been beaten up or been robbed before. He is so in shock that he forgets he has money in the apartment and when it comes back to him he offers it. He says, "I have about 6 thousand dollars here, that's it. Five thousand in an envelope on my dresser and one thousand dollars in my pants pocket on my bedroom floor."

Tears began to fall down his face as he wanted the ordeal to be over with. He begged for his life. "Take the money, that's all I got, just please don't kill me." Aiden watches one of the gunmen enter his room and he looks up at the gunman that's holding the gun on him. That gunman was barking out orders and Aiden was trying to make out the voices. Aiden then feels a blow to the side of his head that gashes his head open. Aiden feels the blood running down the left side of his neck, "Where is the rest at?" yells the gunman that came out holding the envelope and cash. Aiden feels another blow to his forehead this time, creating another gash in his head, blood now running down his face. He is dazed by this blow and he yells, "That's all that I got here, I don't keep any money here. You got all that I got here." The gunman that held the gun on Aiden screamed back. "We're going to kill you if you don't stop lying to us." Aiden said crying, "I swear I don't have any more money here. Just take whatever you want and go, please." The Third man began searching through the apartment and came back with Yogi's jewelry and some Jordan's out of Aiden's closet. Aiden's fears started to turn to anger as he began to recognize the voices he was hearing. He started wondering where Yogi was, was he hiding, or did he leave with Carla, either way, he was glad knowing his brother wasn't experiencing this.

He began second guessing his decision not to go to school like his parents wanted him to. He was getting angry because he had given the gunmen all he had and they still wanted more. He felt his blood running down his face and his neck; He had never felt physical pain like this before. He begins saying a prayer. He mumbled the prayer hoping he would make it out of the situation. His body shivered and his head hurt and then he felt another blow across his jaw and left side of his lip. The blood began building in his mouth, his head now throbbing in pain; he opens his mouth and let the blood pour out. Aiden was upset but feeling defeated. He just wanted this all to end. He didn't want any of it any longer. He didn't want the car, the attention, or the money. He just wanted the gunmen to leave. The gunmen started yelling at each other because two of them were ready to go but the gunman with the gun held on Aiden thought there was more money in the apartment. The gunman said we need to beat his ass until he understands we're not fucking around. Aiden not wanting to take another blow begged for the gunmen to leave. "I don't have any more money here. You have all that I have here. Please just go, I won't call the cops or anything. Just go." The gunmen who originally entered the apartment first, yelled at the gunman holding the gun on Aiden to knock it off, "Let's go." The gunman yelled back "stop being pussy, you're in some gangster shit now, so be gangster, nigga." The original gunman replied, "Yeah, alright," sucking his teeth. Aiden knew the voice and his body filled with anger as he now knew who was doing this to him. He mumbled to himself "I know who you are." The gunmen thought he heard Aiden say something, he was almost sure he heard him say I know who you are. Aiden looked up at the gunman now filled with anger and the next thing Aiden sees is a flash.

surprised Zari by giving her a hundred dollars and told her, "Zari, don't be going anywhere broke, It's cool to let dudes buy you drinks and all that but have your own money to buy them one so they know you a real one too." Zari hugged her sister and smiled before turning to call Carla back and confirm the pickup time.

Zari decided she wasn't spending that money her sister gave her and she wasn't going to allow Carla or Vera to spend money on her for clothes. Zari figured she would just raid her sister Capri's closet. Carpi was the stylish sister of the family. She was an inspiring singer and had so many clothes from her photoshoots and performances. Capri was never home, she was always on the road as either a background singer or as an opening act at some festival. She also performed at jazz bars all over the country. So Zari went into Capri's room and went shopping in Capri's closet. Zari grabbed some ripped jeans and a white top and some yellow heels. She grabs some of her sister's yellow and blue accessories to complete her basketball game fit and grabbed a sexy maxi dresses for any nighttime activities that might take place. She loved to wear maxi dresses because she liked the way her ass would shake wildly as she walked. Although Zari acted as if she didn't like the attention of guys, she really enjoyed being desired the way men desired her sisters. All her life Capri and she would get ignored by all the boys in the neighborhood because of their older sisters whose bodies were more mature. Zari got dressed and headed out of the door to go pick up Carla and Vera.

At the game, Zari notices the scary Mexican man in the stands and he was passionate about Israel's team winning. She just brushed it off thinking it was just a coincidence that she have seen him twice in one day. Israel team lost and Vera was already talking about how upset Israel would probably be and how Tia was going to have to deal with his shit all night now. Zari laughed at the thought but use to have a crush on Israel and once kissed him. She knew Israel wasn't the type of guy she wanted to date but she would wonder what it would be like to be in Tia's shoes from time to time. Carla is always the one plotting seeing Yogi Bear and told the girls to follow her.

Angel was upset and watched as his little sister and her friends talked to that fuck boy, Little Kobe, and his little fat fuck sidekick. Angel notices that Nevaeh's little sister was one of the friends and noticed how much Little Kobe was smiling and trying to get with her. He thought of a plan and took out his phone and called Nevaeh.

Zari and the girls were at the mall. Carla had a few thousand dollars on her and was trying to spend it all. "Damn, bitch! Who the fuck gave you that?" Vera asked excitedly. Carla handed Vera $300 and told her to get her something. Carla reached out her hand to Zari to give her money as well; Zari was going to turn it down but thought she would be closer to paying off her financial aid bill. So she took the money, smiled at her girl, and extended her arms for a hug. Carla happily hugged her friend whom she knew had been having a rough few months. She would do anything to make her "smart" friend better. As the girls held their embrace, Zari's phone begins to ring. It was her sister, Nevaeh, "Hello," Zari answered nervously, thinking her sister was about to ruin her night out and ask for her car back. To her surprised, Nevaeh asked her if she wanted to make some money. "Of course, I do," Zari responded excitedly, "What's up?" Neveah asked her, "Do you remember that dude you saw me talking to?" Zari responded, "The scary-looking Mexican dude, right?" Nevaeh laughed and responded, "yes, well, he said he has seen you at the game talking to someone who owes him money and he wanted to know if you could track that dude for him and when he collects his money from him, he would give you two thousand dollars." "Oh shit, Nevaeh," Zari said surprised, "what do he mean by tracking him, what do I have to do?" Nevaeh said, "Text this number 325-6776 and his name is Angel. He'll tell you what to do. If you're cool with it get that money, if you're uncomfortable about it say No and keep it moving." Zari replied, "Okay, love you, sis. I'll text him and see what he's talking about." Zari hung up the phone and wasn't sure if she should text Angel. He was extremely scary to her but she thought about having Two thousand dollars and how she would have money to pay back what she owes and have money for her pockets. Carla looking at Zari the entire time asked, "What bitch?" Zari smiled at Carla and said that her sister was hooking up a money opportunity for her for a few dollars. Carla understood a few dollars meant a few thousands and hugged her friend again and said, "Good because you need some good shit to happen to you. Now let's go shop, bitch."

Zari and her friends had fun shopping and Zari ended up buying a maxi dress so she could put her sister's dress back. She was sitting in the car looking at her phone trying to decide what to really do. Carla and Vera were smoking and talking about how Yogi and Lil Kobe were looking good. The mention of Lil Kobe's name reminded her to call the scary Mexican man. "Can I speak to Angel?" Zari said nervously, a Serious sounding man stated, "Yeah this me? Who is this?" "This is Zari, Neavaeh's little sister," Zari responded. "Oh, I remember you? So let's get started. That basketball kid, I have seen you talking to earlier at the game," Zari looked confused but curious responded, "Yeah, I know who he is, what do I got to do?" Angel grew excited as he instructed Zari on when to contact him and how she needed to get close to Lil Kobe so he could collect his money from him. Zari was a little concerned about not wanting to be a part of anyone getting hurt. She asked Angel if he planned to hurt Aiden because she didn't feel comfortable with someone getting hurt. Angel somewhat irritated by Zari's question and the fact she was using little Kobe's real name, humanizing him, responded rudely, "Look little homie, you want to get this money or not. Your sister told me you needed some money, so are you down or what?" Zari not wanting to miss out on the money; shook off her concerns and told Angel she was down.

Zari looked at herself in the mirror at Carla's house. She liked the image she saw in the mirror. The yellow maxi dress she had bought with Carla's money hugged her frame just right. It enhanced her features just right. She wasn't sure how the night would play out but she was getting excited about making two thousand dollars. She knew getting close to Aiden would be easy because of their interaction from earlier, she just needed to play it cool and let things happen, and when they would be alone, make up a reason to leave and text Angel and collect her money that night. Vera broke Zari's thoughts when she came in and asked her to take her home. Zari looked puzzled and asked Vera why she was leaving and not going to the party. Vera smiled and got close to Zari and whispered, "You know that thing you got to do tonight for Angel." Zari tightened her face in confusion, "How do you know about that, Vera?" Zari asked. Vera whispered, "Angel is my oldest brother." Vera hugged Zari and said, "Your secret is safe with me, girl. Welcome to the family." Zari had always heard that Vera and Israel had an older brother but never seen him in person and had no idea what he looked like or what his name was. She was disturbed by this last-minute information about this being Vera's brother but the idea of having the money had more of a pull on her mindset at the moment and she again pushed any concerns she had to the back of her mind and smiled at her shape and told herself, *"There's no dude that can resist me today."*

Carla and Zari arrived at the party and it was packed. The parking lot of the apartment was a party on its own. People blasted music from cars and dudes were sitting on cars drinking liquor straight out of the bottle. The smell of marijuana was so strong you would think they walked into a marijuana farm. The women were beautiful and the men were stylish and shooting their shots. Some people were off in their own little cliques, just lounging around like they were tailgating at a football game. Aiden and Yogi definitely were popular, Zari thought to herself. Zari noticed people from high school she hadn't seen in forever, she also noticed some of the sister's friends, ex-boyfriends, and secret lovers. What was so great about the party was the neighbors were out partaking in the festivities. Nobody was complaining about the people or the noise. One neighbor even had his grille out selling BBQ dinners. Zari noticed it and respected the hustle which got her back focus on the task at hand. She followed Carla up the stairs and into Aiden's apartment. Zari took out her phone and texted Angel the address and Aiden's apartment number and put her phone away before Carla noticed. Zari looked up to notice Carla getting a lot of love from guys at the party and just watched the way Carla controlled her environment. Zari wonders how many of these dudes were giving Carla money and how many of them did she let fuck her. Carla was the life of party no matter where she was at. People gravitated to her; she was always the center of attention and not on purpose. Carla was on a mission though, she walked by dudes that I know she would normally give attention to and searched the room with her eyes for something or someone. When she noticed Yogi, she made a straight line to him and Zari followed because she knew Aiden wouldn't be too far away from Yogi. Zari felt her phone vibrating and checked it and it was Angel responding letting her know to text him when things were dying down at the party. She was responding "k" when she heard Aiden's voice, "Excuse me miss, can you help me find this curly hair beauty..."

Zari felt nervous hearing Aiden's voice so she tried to stay cool and looked up from her phone and figured she would play along with Aiden's little game. He smiled at her and Zari noticed for the first time how pretty his teeth were and how he didn't have one pimple or blemish on his skin at all. *Aiden was indeed handsome,* she thought. She danced with him and he had on creed cologne which was a weakness to her. She felt herself becoming attracted to him more and more as the night went on. She hadn't had sex since the nerd fuck boy had played her. While dancing with Aiden, he grabbed her waist and she began imagining him holding on to her waist and pulling her back onto his dick while he hit it from the back; doggy position.

Zari bites her bottom lip which was a thing she did when she was deep in thought. Aiden said something to her; it was all inaudible except the words "stay over." She thought about her task at hand and she was thinking about what reason she would tell Angel for the delay. Zari was making Aiden think she was thinking about telling him yes or no but she was really thinking of what to tell Angel. She had already decided she was going to fuck Aiden. Hell the way she seen it at this point, she was getting the money, she might as well get the dick too. She thought of what to tell Angel and told Aiden yes, Aiden had already told Yogi to kick everybody out. Zari locked eyes with Carla and gave a head nod to her as she was led to Yogi's room for sex. Zari walked into Aiden's room thinking *"I hope his dick is not little and I hope he knows how to use whatever he got."* Zari was proud of herself because of how calm she was in the moment. Zari is really shy and normally gets really quiet and nervous when sex is about to happen. But this was different, Aiden's energy was calming and when he began kissing her she felt her pussy get wet and she got wetter and wetter the closer his kisses got to her pussy. He began to lick on her clit. She closed her eyes and lost herself in the moment. Aiden ate Zari until climax and her climax was strong and relaxing. Aiden put a condom on and allowed Zari to see him for a second. Zari was thinking to herself, *"Oh, he's cool, I can work with that."* She began to anticipate him putting his dick in her and she tensed up a little and squeezed his arms as he slowly inserted himself in her. He began to stroke her and it felt good to her. She wanted to tell him to flip her over and hit it from the back the way she had envisioned earlier but his stroke was so good to her she didn't want to mess up the flow. She noticed him staring at her, trying to lock eyes with her. She opened her eyes to return the stare. The thought ran across her mind, *"Oh, shit, this nigga like me, like me."* Zari smiled at him and bite her lip as she thought about her and him becoming something for real and how she needs to cancel the shit with Angel. She focused her thoughts back on the sensation she was feeling and moan as passionately as she could to let him know she was enjoying him. Zari wrapped her legs around Aiden and locked her feet. She was thinking she was glad he had on a condom or she might've been pregnant again the way he was fucking her. The closer he got to ejaculating the more he moaned and the deeper he fucked her. Aiden getting so close to ejaculating excited her; she was turned on by his sound and how he was losing control of his body. When he finally ejaculated, she was feeling like she had just won the pussy championship of the world. He collapsed on top of her and kissed her neck. Zari told Aiden she had to leave and got up to put her clothes on. She really wanted to text Angel and tell him she wasn't doing it but had already got threaten earlier when she tried that. She was feeling Aiden aka little Kobe and wish she hadn't agreed to let Angel know when Aiden was alone. She checked her phone to see if Carla or her sister had texted.

Zari had four missed text messages. One of the messages was from her sister, Nevaeh, who was just checking on her. Zari responded quickly and replied, "I'm good, having a great time love you, Sis." The other three were from Carla, one giving sexual instructions for Zari, "First when you suck his dick, go down deep as you can on it and suck hard when you coming up, but don't take it out of you're mouth unless you're just teasing him. You want your head to feel like another pussy." Zari laughed to herself reading Carla's tips. The second text message from Carla was just letting Zari know she didn't need a ride home her new boo, Yogi bear, was going to drop her off and the third message let Zari know that Carla made it home and asked if she was okay. Zari replied, "I'm good and I didn't suck any dick tonight but I'll use those tips next time, bitch, Lol." Zari looked up from her phone to see Aiden looking at her. *"Damn, he's fine,"* she thought to herself.

After getting dressed and Aiden the perfect gentlemen offered to walk Zari to her car. Zari took her phone out and held it in front of herself and walked a little ahead of Aiden so she could text Angel she was on the way out. She glanced back and notice Aiden staring at her ass and smiled to herself. She thought, "When this is all over I'm going let him have this ass as much as he can handle." For a split second she thought about tipping Aiden off and letting him know about Angel coming to collect money he owes him but thought differently of it. She sat in her car and Aiden asked her to come back over so they can chill some more. Zari was happy and thrilled he seemed to really be into her. She noticed Aiden break his stare from her and looked towards the parking lot. She wanted to tell him to get in the car and pull off but Aiden quickly said goodbye and left without giving her a kiss or hug. She looked in her side mirror to see Aiden reach the top of his stairs and leave her view. She looked back towards the parking lot and saw two men running towards her. Zari's heart began to race and she felt like she could hear the beating in her chest. As the two men got closer she noticed the scary Mexican man, Angel, and noticed they weren't running just speed walking. Angel gave Zari a head nod and smiled a very evil smile that gave Zari the chills and she turned the key in the ignition and started her sister's car and pulled off. She thought about Aiden and instantly starting to regret the confrontation that he was about to experience. She thought about the evil smile that Angel made and she felt like turning around and going back to interject what was about to happen but she kept driving, she convinced herself the worst that would happen was Aiden and Yogi get into a fight with Angel and that other dude and if he gets beat up she would come over and be his nurse until he got better. She smiled at the idea of that and lied to herself that everything would be okay.

Zari made it home and texted Carla that she made it home. Carla texted back the thumbs up and winking emoji. Zari sent Aiden a text message that she made it home. She hoped he responded quickly but after a few moments, she went into the bathroom to shower. She got out of the shower and checked her phone and still no response from

Aiden. Zari was beginning to get worried. *"Damn, what have I done?"* she asked herself. Just as she was about to get lost in her fears and worries, her sister "The Hazel," walked into their room with two joints rolled up and was like "hey, little sis, I heard you finally got out of the house today." Hazel smiled and offered one of the rolled joints to Zari. Zari took the joint and smiled at her sister and lit the joint and they begin to talk about the mystical powers of the Full Moon.

Zari was awakened from her sleep by the buzzing of her phone. She grabbed her phone and saw she had 22 missed text messages from Carla and 17 missed text messages from Vera. Zari looked at the last message from Carla. It read "BITCH WTF." Zari read all the text messages and begin to panic. Her mind started racing as it starts to set in that something went horribly wrong last night. The last text message she read was sticking to her mind and making her queasy. "Aiden was killed and Yogi is missing." Zari began to feel her heart beating faster, she could hear the pounding of her heart. Perspiration began to form on her forehead. She felt tightness in her chest. Her face tightened as she begins to feel the rush of pain mixed with fear and instant regret all at once. Zari screamed and yelled for her sister, Neveah. "Neveah, Oh my God, what the fuck, Neveah!" Neveah and Zari's, mother, Patricia ran to the room to see what Zari was screaming and yelling about. "What the fuck is wrong with you?" Patricia asked yelling herself. Zari ignored her mother and looked at Neveah, "You heard what happened? Did you hear what they did to Aiden?" Neveah looked at Zari sternly and motion for her to hush by placing her pointing finger over her lips in a pointed up motion. Patricia saw the gesture but acted as if she didn't see it. Zari was crying and looked at her sister and obeyed. Neveah responded to Zari by saying, "He's just a dude that broke your heart in one night. You'll forget about him too." Neveah, only making the statement to throw Patricia off to what Zari was really talking about. Zari screamed, "I'll forget him?" stunned by her sister's comment and she asked again.

"I'll forget him?" Looking confused at her sister. "Yeah, like I said, he was just a boy; you'll meet another one and think you love him too." Neveah turned and walked out of the room, not trying to talk any further about the subject. Zari turned and looked at her mother and saw that Patricia was staring at her, studying her daughter's actions. Zari realized what her mother was doing and wiped the tears from her cheeks and eyes. "I hate boys," she said to her mother, who had a look of disbelief on her face. "I might be a fool but I am no damn fool," said Patricia. Patricia turned to walk out of the room and Zari wanted to tell her mother what had happened as she stared at the back of her mother's head. She wanted to cry in her mother's arms and listen to her mother's voice as she instructed her on what to do about the situation but this one she was going to have to deal with alone.

Zari knew she had to call her friends back to see what happened. So she googled Aiden's name to see what would pop up. Nothing appeared, then she typed in the name of his apartments and she read. "Four people were killed in an apparent robbery gone wrong." Fear began to creep into her mind as she read that police were gathering information about people who were at the party that night. She knew she would be named at some point and need to talk to Neveah so she would know what to do and say. Zari went to Neveah's room which was in the basement of their home. Nevaeh was sitting on the edge of her bed like she was expecting her. Zari stared at her older sister a little intimidated. Neveah had an emotionless, relaxed, calm expression on her face; she rested her right elbow on her right thigh which made her lean forward and to the right and her left arm made a chicken wing with her fist planted into her left hip. She had no shoes on, and at the moment, the only thing that looked girly on her was her white toenail polish on her feet. For the first time, Zari really caught a glimpse of her sister the gangster. Zari tried to speak but stuttered and couldn't get the first word out of her mouth. Neveah cut her off. "Now, Zari, before you start bitching, Fuck them niggas!"

Zari's mouth dropped ajar in disbelief but she just listened to her sister too afraid to interrupt. "Those niggas knew what they were getting into. That little pretty boy you set up was doing too much flossing he made himself hot. He made himself a target the moment he became Whiskey's little money maker and didn't move out of the fucking hood." Nevaeh said boldly. "It's been a few people looking to rob that boy. He was going to get robbed or killed sooner or later. And his dumb ass just pranced around the hood like he was untouchable. Now for Angel and his people, that's just street shit. The streets don't love anybody, anybody can get it. They were sloppy and got caught slipping and that's that." Zari raised her hand to say something like she was in school. "But what about the police, they're going to know I was there. Everybody at the party had seen me and Aiden together the whole night." "They are dead, Zari," Neveah said. The only people that knew about the plot are dead and me and you, right. Zari didn't respond. "So all you gotta say is y'all were together at the party and then you went home. And that's only if they asked. In Which I don't think anyone will," Neveah said convincingly.

Neveah began to talk some more, stating the one issue we have is finding out who killed Angel and his people because clearly, Aiden didn't. Zari begins to wonder who could've killed Angel and his people. Zari begins to feel sad again as she thought about Israel being dead and how the role she played lead to the death of her old crush and her potential love interest, Aiden. Zari glanced back at her sister to be met by her sister's serious stare. "What bitch? What are you so in thought about that you're not listening?" Neveah asked. "I was thinking about people I know dying and who could've killed them. She mentioned that Aiden's best friend, Yogi, is missing but he ain't a killer he definitely would run," said Zari. "Well, somebody killed them so we need to find out who that person is, so if we need to protect you from them we can." Zari hadn't thought about her life being in danger. The fear began to creep into her mind and she stormed out of her sister's room and up the stairs and walked right into her room and rolled up a joint. She began to smoke and laid down on her bed and began to cry. "How could I get myself in this situation?" Zari asked herself. She began to think about all the things she could've done differently that night.

Zari's phone rung, which broke the spell Zari was in and out of her own little self-punishment session. It was Carla. She answered, "Carla, what's up?" "Bitch, what the fuck, I've been calling and texting you all night and morning. Do you know what happened?" Carla asked. Zari not sure what to say just said "No, when I left everything was fine. He walked me to my car after we fucked and I left. I have no clue what happens after that." "Damn, that's fucked up. So don't anybody know what happened to Yogi Bear, either?" asked Carla. "Not that I'm aware of," said Zari. Carla was about to ask another question and then Vera was calling in. Zari told Carla she would call her back because she needed to take the call that was coming in. Carla said, "Alright, but call me back Zari we need to see what the fuck happened." Zari said okay and clicked over to Vera. Vera was speaking in a low assertive voice," "did you warn them niggas that my brothers were about the rob them?" "Hell naw!" Zari said, "I did exactly what Angel told me to do. I didn't even know Israel was with Angel." Vera smacked her lips and said, "Whatever, I know you set my brothers up for that fuck nigga bitch!" Zara was stunned and confused at the tone in which Vera was speaking to her. "Vera, what the fuck, I would never do anything to hurt Israel and you know that," Zari said. Vera didn't believe Zari and told Zari, "Well, bitch, I think you warned those niggas and they killed my brothers, so watch your back, bitch, I'm coming for you!" Vera hung up the phone and Zari began to cry and begin to get frustrated. She headed back to her sister's room, wiping the tears from her cheek and her sister was now lying on her bed smoking. "Nevaeh, we got a problem," said Zari.

TIA

Tia was frustrated with Israel as she stormed out of his mother's home. Tia ignored Israel's mother as she went out of the front door and walked in between Angel and his little flunky cousin. She wanted to let it be known she didn't give a fuck about his family and their thoughts. She held on tight to her son and walked fast to a car that was running and waiting for her. As Tia approached the car she was hoping that Israel would come rushing through the front door to stop her but as she grabbed the door handle she realized he wasn't coming to stop his family from leaving. She began to get irritated with the thought and didn't look back at the house to give Angel the satisfaction in knowing she was looking for Israel to come through the door. She knew she was going to hear her mother's mouth as she got in the car but she would rather deal with her mother's mouth than to sit in the house looking stupid, waiting for Israel and all her wasted planning for the night. "I told you not to move in with that racist ass family," Tia's mother said sarcastically. "Dang, mom, let me get your grandchild in the car good enough before you start with your mess," Tia said.

Tia rode in the car in silence, listening to her mother go on and on about what Tia should've done and what she should do now. " You should just get your own place and I promise, if you put yourself first, that little boy would be at your place every day so you wouldn't have to wait on him to see that y'all need y'all own place now and not when he sees fit. " Tia's mother said in a calm but serious tone. Tia just listened and although she didn't want to hear it her mother was making some sense. She could just go ahead and get a place a one bedroom apartment. She thought about calling her homegirl to see if she can get the waitress job at the strip club.

Tia was at her mom house, in her old room, laying in her bed checking her phone every two minutes to see if Israel had called or texted. He hadn't done either. She let out a deep sigh and thought more about what her mother had said. *"I should just get my own place and force his hand. If I work at the club it would be nights and my son could stay with my mom until I get off or with Israel. I have to make some shit happen too, I'm a queen,"* Tia thought to herself. *"I'm not going sit around and just wait for him like his little pet dog waiting at the door for his return."* she continued in thought. Tia texted her close friend, Nakala, Nakala called instead of responding via text. "Hey, girl, what's up?" Nakala said sounding excited to her from Tia. "I was wondering if you still could get me that job at the club, I need to get my shit together," Tia said. "About damn time," Nakala said really excited about what she was hearing from her friend. "I'm going to the club tonight so meet me there so I can introduce you to Cesar, I told him all about you and how you would be a great bottle girl or maybe even a bartender like me." Tia was still doubtful about working at the club even though Nakala made it seem so exciting. Tia couldn't help but think of how disappointed Israel would be. She checked her phone again and still no text or call from him. "Alright, girl, let me let my mom know so she can watch my son and I'll meet you there," Tia said while sighing. "Yay," said Nakala. "You're about to start getting this money now girl. Are you ready for your life to change?" Nakala asked. Tia didn't answer her and just said, "See you later homie," and ended the call. She laid back on her bed and thought to herself *"This bitch is acting like she's giving me the winning lottery numbers or something,"* and chuckled at the thought.

Tia told her mom she was leaving and asked if she could borrow her car to see about a potential job as a customer service representative. Tia's mom just waved her off and rolled back over to go to sleep. Tia arrived at the bar; Nakala was waiting for her at the door with a skin-tight cheetah print boy cut shorts romper that had openings that exposed her hips and her shoulders. Tia was thinking she didn't remember Nakala's body being that banging. Nakala saw Tia checking her body out and was like "Yasss, bitch! a trip to see Dr. Atlanta got a bitch body together. Now I eat right and stay in the gym so I don't lose my investment." Tia smiled and said, "You look super good girl." Nakala reached out to Tia for a hug and they embraced. The bouncer, a grizzly bear looking man with a beard that didn't connect that was staring at the ladies asked Nakala if Tia was going to work at the bar. Nakala responded, "Yeah maybe." The bouncer rubbed his hands together and said "I hope so." As If Tia was Thanksgiving food prepared by his mother. Tia felt uncomfortable at how comfortable he was saying this aloud. Tia thought about Israel and his disapproval of her being there. She checked her phone again to see if he had called or texted, but he hadn't. Tia began to get worried, this wasn't like her man. She began to call him and began scrolling to his name so she could complete the call and then she was interrupted by a deep voice, "Hello, I'm Tyree."

Tia was startled but regained her composure and stop looking at her phone and looked to see who was introducing himself to her. Standing in front of her was a tall man with a football player neck and shoulders with his hair slicked back in a ponytail Steven Segal style. He had a thin trimmed mustache and goatee. He talked with a rhythm like he was about to start singing or rapping. He sounded like the sixth member of Bone Thugs and Harmony. Standing next to him was Nakala, smiling from cheek to cheek. Seeing her smile relaxed Tia and Tyree continued with his introduction. "My bad, I didn't mean to scare you. I'm Tyree but everybody calls me Ty and I'm the night manager here at the bar. Nakala speaks highly of you and believes you'll be an asset here to our team. She also believes we can be a great benefit for you as well." Tia smiled and the light gleamed on Tia's face at the same time and Tyree saw the beauty that Nakala had told him about. A lot of thoughts begin to go through Tia's head. *"Why he talks like a pimp?"* *"Israel's going to kill me."* Tia snapped out of it in enough time to get out some questions for Tyree. She asked him how this place could be helpful for her. Tyree began to give Tia the positives of working there and never gave her the negatives of working at the bar but Tia had a sense of what the negatives would be. Tia told Tyree she just wanted to Hang out for the night and catch the vibe of the place and see if she would be comfortable. Tyree told her cool and to hang out with Nakala and reach out to him if she had any questions. Tia said cool and turned to walk towards the bar where Nakala was at making drinks. Tia could feel the stares as she walked towards the bar. She turned back towards Tyree to catch him watching her walk and she thought to herself, *"Damn, can I really do this?"* Nakala saw the facial expressions on Tia's face and said, "Girl, you'll get use to it, after a while you won't even notice the stares." Tia smiled and Nakala handed her a drink, "vodka and cranberry, right?" Nakala asked. The drink made Tia think of Israel and she checked her phone to see if he had called or texted. She hadn't heard anything from her man and Israel didn't have any social media accounts.

Tia texted Israel and sent "Hey, bae, I miss you, and where you at?" Tia sat the phone down on the bar and made small talk with Nakala and checked her phone periodically. When she didn't get any responses from Israel she began to worry more as the night came to an end. Tia noticed that Nakala had made over one thousand dollars in one night and Tia was sold. Tia told Nakala she was about to leave and that she would call her tomorrow to set up a meeting with Tyree about starting there. Nakala smiled and Tia headed to her mother's car. Once Tia got to the car she wanted to ride by Israel's house to see what was up with her man.

Tia rode by the house and saw that nobody was outside in front of the house. Angel and his goons were normally outside at all times of the night. She pulled up to the house and walked to the side door. Israel's mother opened the door and said, "He's not here, he is gone with his brother doing what real men do," and slammed the door closed in

Tia's face. Tia could feel the anger building up and she thought fuck Israel and stormed back to her mother's car.

Tia cried the entire drive back to her mother's house. *"How could Israel go out and do some stupid shit with his dumb ass brother?"* she thought. "So, fuck his son and I, he's just going to risk going to jail for something we don't really need, just to feed his egos," she yelled angrily. Tia was so upset and wanted to calm down. She went to her mother's refrigerator and took a bottle of Riunite wine and took it back to her room and began to drink it straight out of the bottle. She begins to laugh at the thought of her drinking the wine bottle like she was drinking a forty-ounce beer like Regina King as Shalika from the movie Boys N the Hood. She thought to herself she better go get a wine glass, she thought she looked stupid. Tia took her clothes off so she could take a shower and wash the bar scent off her body and out of her hair. She poured a glass of wine and took it to the bathroom with her. She sipped on the wine as she let the water get a hot as she could stand it. She kept thinking about Israel and wondering if he was going to call when he got done doing whatever he was doing. She was hoping he would just show up at her mother's house but the thought faded as she was thinking about him and how he hadn't reached out to her which made her upset some more. She sat her glass of wine down and enter the shower.

Once Tia finished showering she had two towels, one wrapped around her body and the other wrapped around her head. She poured some more wine and sat on the bed, thinking about how to make her future work with or without her man. She thought about how she could work at the bar and make some real money and get the apartment on her own and Israel would come over anyway so he would be there and follow her plan without all the delay. She thought yeah he will be happy once we're there and he'll see that I was right. We don't need a lot of money to move we just need to do it. She downed the rest of the wine she had in her glass and laid down on her bed looking at the ceiling. She checked her phone one last time and he still hadn't responded to her message. She texted him, "I love you Israel and we can talk about your rough day tomorrow. I hope we can have a do-over and you let me make you feel better about losing that game today. I miss you like crazy; one day apart is too many. Good night my King, come get your family as soon as possible. Love you." Tia closed her eyes and thought to herself, *"No matter what I'm going make tomorrow a better day,"* and she dozed off to sleep still wrapped in her towels.

Whiskey

Whiskey pulled onto his street and as he got closer to his home, he noticed the truck he gave Yogi sitting in front of his home. The truck was running with the music blasting loudly. "What the fuck is he doing?" Whiskey scoffed. Whiskey parked his burgundy corvette at the end of the driveway, grabbed his 45 automatic handgun from his hip, and slowly walked towards the driver side door with his eyes squinted and focused, looking for any sudden movement. Whiskey got to the door and realized Yogi was slumped over with his head against the driver's side window, Whiskey wasn't sure if Yogi was dead or sleep drunk. He tapped on the window with the barrel of his gun but Yogi didn't move. Whiskey reached for the door handle to see if the door would open and it did. The door flung open waking Yogi up some. Yogi began mumbling "they killed him" "they killed him" repeatedly. Whiskey could barely hear Yogi but he made out what Yogi was saying and he noticed Yogi's bloody hands. "Who did they kill, Yogi?" asked Whiskey calmly, knowing it could be only one person Yogi was referring to. "My brother, my motherfucking brother," Yogi cried. Whiskey dropped his head and lowered his gun. Whiskey had been around death a lot in his life and became numb to it a long time ago as a youth. He placed his hand on Yogi's shoulder and asked Yogi in a stern voice, "What are you going to do about it?"

Yogi began to raise his head for the first time and was met with a cold-hearted malicious stare from Whiskey. Yogi mumbled, "I killed them, Whiskey, but I have a few people to get." Whiskey nodded his head in approval of what Yogi just said and told Yogi to pull that truck in the back of the house and come inside so they can talk. Yogi did as he was told. Whiskey saw the situation as a plus, he thought it was a shame what happened to Aiden but figure he could use Yogi in a bigger role in his operation. Whiskey knew he could use Yogi's rage to help his organization. Whiskey needed a killer on his staff that he could mold and Yogi was going to be the perfect person. Yogi entered Whiskey's home for the first time. Yogi notice how nice everything was but wasn't in the mood to pay closer attention. Whiskey called for Yogi to come into the dining room. Yogi walked in and saw Whiskey sitting at a large black marble table and already had Yogi's chair pulled out with his hand gesturing for Yogi to sit down. Yogi sat down, never lifting his eyes up towards Whiskey. Whiskey began speaking in his deep voice, leaning back in his chair, pouring whiskey into his coffee. "Yogi, I know you're hurting and you probably never thought this day would happen but it did. Now I don't know what happened and I don't want to know." This statement made Yogi change his depressed, defeated stare to a more serious confused look on his face. Whiskey continues, "This pain you're feeling is a gift, now you can be like these weak motherfuckers out here and let that pain break you or you can use it to become a real man. You can use this to be the man everyone fears like me." Yogi was listening attentively but could feel the rage rising up the back of his neck. Whiskey leaned in towards Yogi and started speaking through his teeth, "make all these motherfuckers pay, anybody that opposes you, anybody that's not on your team, and anybody that's stopping you from getting what you want. Make them all pay for what happened to Aiden. Let me help you become the man Aiden needed you to be so you can ensure none of your loved ones ever get hurt again." Whiskey sat back and interlocked his fingers staring at Yogi for a few moments. Whiskey asked Yogi, "Do you want to be the most powerful man in the city?" Yogi nodded his head yes. Whiskey then said, "Let me help you become that, I'll tell you everything you need to know and teach you the game and how to conduct yourself. I'll help you become the beast you were destined to be. Those streets killed your brother and you have to seek revenge on them. You have to go out there and kill everything moving in those streets. You have to conquer them and have them working for you." Yogi was getting pumped up by the way Whiskey was talking to him. Yogi was upset, and although he killed the guys that killed Aiden his hungry for revenge hadn't been fulfilled. Whiskey could see the anger and violence in Yogi's eyes. Whiskey thought to himself *"I got a vampire on my hands and he's out for blood."* Whiskey got up from the table and told Yogi, "You stay with me now." Whiskey told yogi to follow him and guided him to a room in the back of the house. "This is your room, Yogi Bear, I want you to take all the time you need to rest and think about the person you're about to become. You owe it to Aiden; you got my blessing and guidance to do whatever you need to do. You're going to earn more money than you can dream of and you're going to be the most respected man in our city. I'm going to help you get the revenge you seek." Yogi nodded his head without saying a word, he went into the bedroom and closed the door behind, and lay on the bed to cry one last time. Whiskey smiled at the thought of having Yogi on his team as a killer. He knew that type of raw rage was hard to come by. He also knew everything he told Yogi about conquering the streets was some bullshit but he didn't care he just needed Yogi to believe in him and do whatever he needed him to do.

Whiskey laughed to himself at the thought of Yogi being in his house and pulled out his cell phone and dialed a number. It rang a few times before a woman answered, "Hello," the woman answered. "Yeah, this is Whiskey," he said. The woman smacked her lips in irritation, "what the hell do you want?" Whiskey grinned, and began talking slow and boastfully, "You did everything in your power to keep him from me. You did everything you could to make sure he didn't know who I was but guess what? Your GOD delivered him right to my front steps and he's willing to let me teach him how to be a real man. I'm going to teach him my entire quote unquote bad ways. I'm going to teach him about power and how to use who he is to be respected in this world. I told you bitch; you might as well let me raise him from day one. You had him out here living like shit in your mother's raggedy-ass house. I did exactly what you wanted me to do, I stayed away. I didn't interfere with your wishes but I told you one day he would be with me and that day have come." The woman couldn't speak, the phone was dead silent. "Put my baby on the phone, nigga," the woman screamed angrily. "See, that's your fucking problem, he's no fucking baby," Whiskey said in a more serious tone. "See, I ain't shit, I'm a demon out here in this world, I understand who I am, what's fucked up is you don't understand you ain't shit either and you're a demon as well. You laid down and had a baby with a demon because that's what you are attracted to. Then you tried to get all righteous and shit. Well, look at that, what was meant to be will be. And I'm not going to tell him I'm his father because I don't want him to hate you for it, so say thank you." "Fuck you," shouted the woman. Whiskey laughed and said, "I knew you still had a thing for me." The woman began to shout at Whiskey and he ended the call without saying anything and chuckled at her anger and frustration. Whiskey walked back to the dining room and sat in the chair to finish his coffee, amused and pleased with himself. He enjoyed pissing people off. Whiskey sat there at the table sipping his coffee staring out of the window, thinking of how great life is. Yogi was standing in the bathroom doorway stunned. He had heard everything Whiskey was saying on the phone. His anger began to grow even more and he quietly ducked back into his room.

ZARI

Zari was sitting on the living room couch patiently, waiting for her sister to come home. She needed to talk to Nevaeh about how to handle the Vera situation. Patricia, Zari's mother, was watching Zari and thinking to herself why her Zari looked so nervous and how she needed to find out what was going on. Patricia was watching the first 48 detective TV show on her television which seemed to be watching Patricia more than her watching it because she couldn't keep her eyes off her daughter and studying her behavior. Patricia broke the silence between her and her daughter. "You know your sister is home from off the road, She got a few music deal contracts to look at. She may sign a deal this time." This information woke Zari out of her trance and she stood and rushed to see her sister, Capri. "Capri, Capri," yelled Zari. "Hey, Baby girl, relax; I'm in here." Zari opens her sister's door and saw Capri lying on her bed. Zari jumped in the bed with her almost causing them to fall out of it together. They laughed as they hugged each other. "How have you been, little sister?" Capri asked. "I've been going through it but I'm much happier to see you now." "How was the road? Are you seriously going to sign a contract and become a star?" Zari Asked. Zari was such a fan of her sister and she couldn't help but be excited to speak to her as if she was speaking to Rihanna. Capri laughed but didn't answer her sister's questions but asked some questions of her own.

"Hey, how are you feeling with that abortion decision you made? Are you good with that? Also, who is the boy that got you taking my clothes and getting dress up for?" The Question brought seriousness back to Zari's demeanor. She had forgotten all about her boy issues until that moment. She looked her sister in the eyes and said, "The baby thing is heartbreaking and the boy was a mistake." Capri looked at her sister with sincere sympathy and began to ask her more questions but as she began to ask, Nevaeh walked into the room.

"Sorry to break up y'all little reunion but mom said you need to talk to me, Zari, What's up?" Zari got off the bed and motion for Nevaeh to follow her. Nevaeh did so and said to Capri jokingly, "The superstar has graced us with her presence." Capri retorted, "Whatever, you wanna be Butch Davis." They shared a laugh and Nevaeh followed Zari, who was headed down to Nevaeh's room. Once Nevaeh enters the room Zari began to explain to her that Vera felt like she set her brothers up and she was going to get at her for it. Nevaeh didn't say a word she just listened to Zari. Zari was sweating and a nervous wreck, she needed to chill out but her sister just watched her and thought to herself, *"I'm getting this little girl back in school, she's a true civilian and not made for anything criminal."* Nevaeh chuckled at the thought. Zari snapped, "What the fuck so funny, Nevaeh?" Nevaeh just responded, "You!" Zari continued ranting, "Let me tell you something, I don't have time for people looking for me and all that." Zari noticed that her sister wasn't even paying her any attention and asked her a question? "What are we going do about Vera?" Nevaeh shrugged her shoulders and said, "We," pointing at her sister and then herself, "we ain't going to do shit. You're going to enroll back in school and get that dream job so you can take care of us." Zari was confused, "But what about Vera?" Zari asked. Nevaeh stated, "She's not your concern, and don't worry about it. Nothing's going to happen to you, so go listen to T.I and be easy." Nevaeh pulled a roll of money out of pocket and asked Zari how much she needed to get back in school. Zari said $900. Nevaeh looked at her funny as if she was lying but gave her $2000 and told her to also get the books she needed. Zari was stunned but extremely happy. Zari began to go back up the stairs when she was met by Patricia at the top of the stairs. "Zari, the police here to speak to you, what the fuck did you do?"

YOGI

Whiskey woke Yogi up real early and told him to get dressed because he had to take him around and introduce him to everybody. Whiskey wanted to let people know that Yogi was his right-hand man now. Yogi's emotions were all over the place. He idolized Whiskey and was in awe of him but learning that Whiskey was his father had him upset that this information was kept from him. Yogi was upset with his mother. Yogi thought about how his adolescence would've been different had everybody known he was Whiskey's kid. Nobody would've teased him and he knows he would've been best-dressed kid and had all the girls he could handle. Yogi glanced at Whiskey; he didn't see any resemblance of himself in Whiskey. Yogi thought maybe he should say something to Whiskey to let him know that he heard the phone call. Yogi wanted to ask Whiskey if he had any other siblings. Aiden begins to flood into Yogi's mind. *"I got a brother already,"* he thought to himself. Yogi's curiosity was replaced with pure anger. Yogi broke the silence, "when do I get a gun and when do I get to hurt somebody?" Whiskey turned and grinned with a surprised look on his face. "Don't worry, you'll get to prove yourself really soon." Whiskey replied, still grinning and nodding his head with excitement. "Good!" Yogi mumbled.

Whiskey pulled up to a house on a street that seemed abandoned as if a war had happened on it and the shell remains of empty houses told the haunting story of the war forgotten about. The few houses that remain intact and occupied were surrounded by weeds and uncut grass with abandoned cars and old furniture in vacant lots. It was a group of Men sitting on the porch of one of those few standing houses. The home was an old ugly home with new windows and security doors. The home had yellow siding and brown trimming around the doors and windows. The siding had become a darker yellow and not the bright yellow it probably once was due to the lack of cleaning over the years it had been neglected. The porch was brown as well and spread across the entire front of the home. So when Whiskey and Yogi pulled up, people were spread across the entire porch. A few of the men stood up as Whiskey's S63 AMG Mercedes Benz came to stop in front of the house. Yogi thought to himself, *"How is that porch holding all those people on it."* The porch was past its prime and needed repairs badly. Whiskey turned to Yogi and handed him SIG Sauer P220 10mm semi auto pistol. Whiskey said to Yogi, "this gun is a throw-away, so if you have to use it get rid of it." Yogi understood and asked Whiskey, "Which one of these dudes I get to test it out on?" Whiskey replied, "If they don't have my money, hit as many as you can."

Yogi's heart started pounding, he could feel it. He began to feel the sweat forming on the back of his neck. Yogi was quietly nervous. Whiskey must have a feel for energy because he reminded Yogi they were dudes like the dudes on that porch that killed little Kobe, his brother. The sound of hearing Aiden's name caused Yogi to squint his eyes and bite down on his teeth. Yogi got out of the car first. Whiskey got out of the car at his regular cool slow pace. Whiskey felt he could think better as long as he kept everything at his pace and not to allow anybody or anything to speed him up. Whiskey mentioned for one of the guys to come to him. A tall guy maybe 6 foot 5inches with a light-skinned tone complexion with a candy corn-shaped head and muscular build came down from the porch and walked to Whiskey. Yogi had his hand on his gun and darted his eyes back and forth from the tall guy and the guys on the porch. The tall dude got right in front of Whiskey and stopped, he glanced towards Yogi and looked him up and down. Yogi stared back at the guy with no break in his stare for a few moments before turning back to the porch. Whiskey announced, "This is Bear, my right-hand man," as if the guy had asked for an introduction. Whiskey waived his point and middle fingers signaling for the guy to get closer to him. The tall guy leaned towards Whiskey and Whiskey whispered something to the guy. Yogi couldn't hear Whiskey but the guy stepped back and said, "I don't have it all," Whiskey sighed and looked at Yogi and said Bear, "light him up." Yogi hesitated for a moment, he gasped and then pulled the trigger hitting the tall guy seven times before turning towards the porch and continuing to shoot. Some of the guys on the porch began jumping off of it, some just dropped down on the porch with their hands above their heads in a submissive position. A woman with a short stature came running out of the house with a black shopping bag, yelling and screaming at Whiskey to take the money.

Whiskey grabbed the black shopping bag with the words thank you on it and began counting the money like he didn't have a care in the world, licking his thumb several times while shuffling between the money that was in his hands. The women dropped to the ground screaming and grabbing at the dying man's shirt. Yogi was staring at the scene shocked at what he just did. Whiskey called "Bear" in his regular low smooth tone. Yogi looked at Whiskey and Whiskey winked. "Muthafucka should've just paid the damn money!" Whiskey calmly said in the direction of the woman who was still screaming and crying for the tall guy bleeding all over the concrete motionlessly. Yogi thought to himself *"He ain't so tall anymore."* Whiskey got in the car and Yogi got in after him. Whiskey put on his shades and pulled off. Yogi was thinking to himself how he liked how "Bear" sounded instead of Yogi or Yogi Bear. Yogi looked behind him to see the aftermath of what just took place. Whiskey asked Yogi, "What are you looking back for?" Yogi responded, "Nothing." Whiskey began talking, "the message was sent, no need to re-check it or check on them."

Yogi relaxed and realized he could never concern himself with other people's hurts, fears, and wants. Moving forward he would be ruthless and focused. Yogi thought to himself that he wouldn't be funny anymore and wanted to be taken serious, dead serious if necessary. Yogi liked Whiskey's confidence and King like attitude. *"But even Kings die."* Yogi sat on the passenger side seat thinking to himself. He wanted to be a GOD, he continued in thought. *"I'm going to be a myth; I'm going to be the nightmare people hoped to avoid."* Whiskey noticed Yogi deep in thought. Whiskey asked, "You good, Bear?" "Did that bother you?" Yogi liked hearing Whiskey calling him Bear. He smiled at Whiskey and said, "I'm going to make you proud of me and hold it down for Aiden and for you. I'm ready to go put in more work." Whiskey stuck his fist out towards Yogi to give him a pound. Yogi raised his fist to meet Whiskey's fist to complete the gesture. Whiskey didn't smile or say anything. He looked at Yogi seriously for a moment and turned his music to his favorite artist Al Green. "Here I am baby; come and take me," the words of Al Green's voice started to calm Yogi down and he began laughing to himself at the thought of two killers riding in the car listening to some 1970s love Ballads.

Yogi looked at Whiskey and smiled and thought to himself, *"Damn bro Whiskey is my dad."* As if he was talking to Aiden. Yogi closed his eyes and laid his head back on the car headrest. Whiskey, out of the blue said, "We won't be seen for a few days we're going stay low. I'm going to teach you different methods for pulling off hits and we'll show up for the basketball game. They're holding a memorial for little Kobe." At that moment Yogi opened his eyes and a flood of emotions rushed him. He instantly thought about Carla and how he needed to talk to her. He wanted to see if she had set him and Aiden up.

Yogi pictured Zari's curly hair and the sundress she had on, it was yellow and she wore a gold chain around her waist that read "QUEEN." The rage began to build up to the point of boiling. Yogi bites down on his teeth in frustration due to the memory of Zari giving a head nod to the men that killed his brother. Yogi asked Whiskey if he could get him boxing lessons, Whiskey said, "Yeah, I sure can." Yogi closed his eyes again and imagined himself beating

Zari to death with his bare hands.   Whiskey broke Yogi's thoughts. "Hey, Bear, you feel like making another run?" Yogi mumbled, "Hell, yeah, promise me I get to hurt someone." Whiskey smirked and said, "Maybe." Yogi closed his eyes and prepared his mind to curve his weakness and embrace the monster he would be moving forward in life. Al green was still singing in the background. Yogi's memories took him back to the scene of the 3 dead men laying on top of each other as he came up the stairs to see his brother's body folded over on itself. He remembers the last person he shot trying to talk and him not really hearing anything, just him pulling the trigger and thinking about how his brother was looking bad and he failed him. Yogi rode the rest of the car ride in silence with his eyes closed. If he was alone he might've cried but he fought the urge to cry. He told himself he would never cry again.

Whiskey broke Yogi out of his trance when he came to a stop and turned the music down. "Bear, Bear!" Whiskey called to Yogi, "I need you to come in here with me, I need to introduce you to some people so they know you will be collecting money for me moving forward." Yogi open his eyes a little disappointed that this didn't seem like the kind of run that he would get a chance to take some of his frustrations out. Yogi got out of the car and walked towards a pool hall that looked like it was just remodeled. The pool hall windows and doors had security bars on them. When Yogi entered the building behind Whiskey, there were three large bouncers at the door that stopped Yogi, Yogi frowned his face in disgust and Whiskey looked back and said, "He's with me" and the bouncers raised their hands and let Yogi by. Whiskey looked back again and told the bouncers, "that's my guy, he always good from now on."   The bouncers acknowledge Whiskey's statement and nodded to Yogi in an unspoken apology. Yogi acknowledge with a head nod in return. Whiskey had walked to a pool table in the middle of the room where some people were just standing around as if they were waiting for

82

him. He waived for Yogi to catch up to him. Yogi sped up and caught up and Whiskey began introducing Yogi to everybody around. No one said a word they all just looked at Whiskey attentively. Nothing stood out about the group of people at this pool table. None of them was flashy, some were old men, some younger men but one person did stand out because she was a female and seemed to be the youngest person in this crew until Yogi got there. She caught Yogi staring at her and starred back for a few seconds before turning back to Whiskey. Yogi felt weird staring at her. She was beautiful but she was dressed like a tomboy. She stood there with her beautiful soft face with a tattoo over her right eyebrow that read "HUSTLE" and Yogi laughed at the thought that he was attracted to a possible stud and she seemed to notice that he was staring and thinking something. She broke her attention from Whiskey again and stared at Yogi with her tough face as to say "what" without saying a word. Yogi nodded his head and turned his attention back to Whiskey. Whiskey then said, "This is Bear, he's my right hand now and you will call him when you need something and he will do the pick-ups." They all acknowledge without saying a word and Whiskey said, "I'll provide his number to y'all in a few days." The group went their own way and went back to whatever pool game they must've been playing before Whiskey got there. Whiskey called to Yogi and said I want you to meet someone and the tomboy that Yogi had been admiring stuck her hand out and said, "Hey, I'm Nevaeh."

ZARI

Zari's heart skipped a beat as she walked to the top of the stairs and past her mother into the living room where two detectives were standing waiting for her. They had serious, unforgiving looks on their faces as one detective looked her up and down and the other looked all around the living room. She understood they were looking for signs of anything. As she got closer to the detective that was looking her up and down, she looked up to meet her eyes and extended her hand to Zari. "Za..Zari, is it?" asked the detective, struggling to pronounce Zari's name. "Yes," Zari said tentatively, barely audible. "Well, I'm detective Green and this is Detective McCarthy and we have a few questions for you." "About what?" Zari asked looking back at her mother with a confused looked on her face. Neveah was just walking in the living room at this point and gave a slight head nod to Zari and leaned against the wall. Patricia noticed the exchange between her daughters but turned her attention back to Detective Green with a warrior's stare. Detective McCarthy an older chubby man in his mid to late fifties continued looking around the room and watching Neveah and Patricia with accusatory eyes. Detective Green maintained her focus on Zari and stated, "I would like to ask you about your whereabouts last night, were you at a party on the west side of town Last night?" Zari looked back to Neveah who just returned a stare and raised her left eyebrow. Detective Green broke her stare at Zari to look at Neveah and Neveah returned the stare at Detective Green. Neveah instantly looked at the detective's braids and thought to herself, *"she needs to let me touch that up, she probably had those braids in for 3 months or more."* Detective Green noticed Neveah sizing her up and cleared her throat and brought Neveah's eyes back to hers. Detective Green turned back to Zari and looked at her waiting for Zari to address the questions asked. Zari turned and looked at Patricia and Patricia said, "Go on and answer the questions Zari, I don't want these people in my house all day." Zari return her attention to the detective and said, "I went to a party on the west side."

Detective Green asked Zari, "did you go to the party by yourself, or were you with someone." Zari replied she went to the party by herself. Detective Green then said, "We interviewed several people at the party that night, and people saw you there with other people." Zari stated,"Of course, it's a party I wasn't going to be in a party and not talk to anybody." Patricia interrupted, "Detective, before you continue asking my baby these questions, do you want to tell us what this is about first." Detective Green looked back at Detective McCarthy he gave a nod of approval. Detective Green turned to Zari and said, "This is the concerning the murder of Aiden Smith-Ali." "Murder," Patricia said stunned. "My baby didn't murder anybody." Detective Green interrupted, "we're not saying she did but we're hoping she can give us more information about the party and if she noticed anything strange. She was with the decease most of the night even after the party ended according to witnesses." Patricia looked at Zari and then looked at Neveah with disgust. By this time Zari's two other sisters, Capri and Hazel, were in the living room listening to what was going on. Zari broke the silence and stated, "He was fine when I left him. I just met him that day earlier at a basketball game and he invited me to his party. So I went and I left a little after the party was over. He was fine when I left said, he was about to go to bed."

Detective Green asked Zari about the basketball game and asked if a young lady name Vera Rodriguez was with her. Zari said, "Yes, she was at the game, her brother was playing in the game as well." Detective then turned the line of questions about Vera, "How well did you know Ms. Rodriguez? Did she know about the party? Did she have any issues with Mr. Smith-Ali?" Zari started feeling like she was in the twilight zone. She started sweating and losing control of her breathing. The weight of what happened the night before began to weigh her down. She began breaking down, Neveah notice and put her arms around her youngest sister and said, "It's okay, we're here for you." Zari began answering the questions and asked the detective why she wanted to know all this information about Vera. Detective Green then said, "Well, Ms. Rodriguez, was found died today and three of her relatives were found at the scene of the crime dead. So we are trying to find out why Ms. Rodriguez's family would want to do something to Mr. Smith-Ali and who would want her dead and was it linked to the deaths of her relatives." Zari's mind was blown, tears began to form in her eyes and she couldn't help them from falling. "Vera is dead?" she asked. She began shaking and she couldn't believe what she was hearing. Vera had been her friend since childhood. She thought she would be able to talk to Vera and they'll work through what happened. She never thought about losing Vera.

The guilt of her decision began beating her down, she collapsed to the ground crying uncontrollably and Patricia told the detectives that Zari wouldn't be answering any more questions. Hazel began crying and picked her sister up and began walking her back to the room that they shared. Capri turned and followed her sisters. Neveah and Patricia stared at each other and back to the detectives. Patricia began telling the detective that Vera and Zari had been friends since elementary school and this news is just too shocking for them right now. Detective handed her card to Neveah and asked them to call her if they find out any helpful information. Neveah didn't say a word or look at the card. Patricia showed the detectives to the door and watched them pull out of her driveway and drive away from her home. Patricia turned to Neveah and said, "You're going to tell me what the fuck is going on, Neveah." Neveah looked at her mom and said, "Nothing I can't handle," and turned to walk away. Patricia grabbed her shoulder and said, "Listen, you little bitch, don't forget who you're talking to. You're going tell me what the fuck is going on. I know Vera's brother was over here for you and I also know Zari has been a complete wreck since this morning. She got here last night happy and floating around here like a butterfly, like she had the fuck of her life and then she crying and sad all fucking day having these little meetings with you and you sitting around here unbothered . You're going to tell me what the fucks up or we're going to be a house full of fighting bitches today." "Alright mom, I'll tell you but you got to relax," said Neveah. Neveah asked Patricia to go for a ride with her and she would bring her up to speed.

VERA

Vera was thinking to herself how happy she was to be at the mall with Zari and Carla. Zari was Vera's best friend and she really enjoyed their journey. Carla was her friend too but she wasn't as close to Carla as she was to Zari. Carla had just given her some money to buy some new clothes which she needed. Vera was slightly jealous of the way Carla got to enjoy different men the way she did. Vera had a hard time getting and keeping a boyfriend of any kind due to her brothers' harassment of any male that showed her any attention. Vera was excited about the party and was hoping she would meet someone she liked. Vera had decided someone was about to get that work tonight. She hadn't been intimate in about 6 months and was on edge. She found her a form-fitting black dress. She didn't have Carla's video curves or Zari uniqueness but she understood how to be sexy and although she wasn't the popular one of their crew she garnished her fair share of attention from men. She was confident and knew black guys couldn't get enough of her although she hadn't been with a black guy before. She decided tonight would be the night. She wanted the freedom to date whomever she wanted. Her brothers were allowed to date whomever they wanted but she had not, and tonight would be the day she lived her truth and lived her life as she saw fit. The girls were having fun and they talked about how good they were going to look tonight and Vera told Zari her plans to sleep with a black guy and Zari was confused. "Bitch, I thought you been doing that?" Vera laughed and said, "No, but tonight it was going down." They shared a laugh. Then Vera's phone rang, it was her oldest brother, Angel, and she prepared to hear his mouth and complaints about something he didn't like. Vera answered the phone with an attitude. "What!" Angel, always direct with his speech, got right to the point. "Hey, little sis, you can't go to the party." "What the fuck, why not?" asked Vera in her really low voice. "Angel, your friend, Zari, is about to help the family set that little Kobe dude up so we can get all that money he has been getting and help Israel move into his own place." Vera was disappointed but she also put her family first in most matters. She understood how bad her brother wanted to get him and Tia their own place. She also understood she would have his room if he moved out and she could move out of her mother's room. She dropped her sadness; her black guy lust night would have to wait. This was family and family comes first.

Vera smiled at the idea that Zari was helping her family. She thought to herself she's my family for real. Vera asked Zari to drop her off. Vera whispered something to Zari which shocked Zari. Vera didn't say much on the car ride home. She began to daydream about getting her brother's room and she was going to decorate it and finally have her own. Vera was snapped out of her daydreaming by the sound of Carla's voice, "Hey, Bitch, where the fuck are you right now?" Zari and Carla began laughing. Vera realized the car was no longer moving and was in front of her house.

She smiled at the girls and told the girls to have fun and fuck a cute nigga for her. Zari asked her if she was sure she couldn't come to the party. Vera said, "Naw, I better sit this one out." Vera smiled and winked at Zari. Vera got out of the car walked into the house right past her mother to the room that they shared, she peeked in the room and turned around and walked to Israel and Tia's room, peeked in there and turned, and walked back to the living room and sat next to her mother and asked, "Where is Izzy at?" "Tia and your brother got into it and Tia left with the baby," her mother said, without looking up from the TV. "Oh, dang, did you cook mom?" Vera asked. "It's on the stove," Vera's mom said. Vera got up and went into the kitchen to make her a plate, as she was warming her food up in the microwave, she could smell the pork chops, red beans, and rice. As she sat down to eat her food her brothers and her cousin came into the kitchen dressed in all black clothing. Israel looked at Vera and just nodded his head at her and waited for his brother and cousin. Vera's cousin didn't speak; he just walked past Israel and went out of the side door. Angel pulled a chair in front of Vera and asked her how Zari was acting. Vera replied, "She was acting normal, she's good." Angel said, "That's good, I'm going to give you some of the money for not going to that party tonight." Vera was excited, she thought little Kobe and Yogi were cool but they weren't family. Angel kissed Vera on her forehead and walked out of the door. Vera called Israel's name, he turned around and she said, "Don't worry about Tia and Izzy, Y'all will all be together in your own place after you handle your business tonight." Israel smiled and headed out of the door. Vera washed the dishes and flopped down on the couch to watch TV with her mother. Her mother was smoking a joint, laughing, and slapping her knee at the TV show she was watching. Vera laughed at her mother and curled up on the couch and began to doze off to sleep.

Vera was awakened by her mother shaking her and screaming her name, "VERA, VERA, VERA, WAKE UP BABY, WAKE UP!" "What's up, Shit mom," Vera said barely audible. "They found four dead bodies at that apartment," her mother said frantically. "What apartment?" Vera asked more alert now. Vera's mother continued, "The apartment Angel went to help Israel." "How do you know those are the apartment's mommy?" Vera asked now in a panic state. "Because Angel tells me all his plans in case something goes wrong." Vera's mother said almost in tears. Vera began to fear the worst and began to dial numbers on her phone. Her mother now standing up and pacing back and forth, smoking a cigarette, seen Vera dialing numbers and asked confused, "What are you doing, Vera?" Vera replied, "Calling Angel." "No Vera, Angel said never call if something happens because they keep their phones in the car." Her mother continued, "Vera, we got to go there and get the car." Vera mother grabbed her by her shirt and they rushed out of the house.

There were police and onlookers everywhere. Vera's mother spotted the car and said, "That's it, let's get it and get out of here." Vera didn't respond, she wanted to see if it was really her brothers. She got out of her mother's car and began walking towards the apartments and her mother grabbed her by the shoulder, "Snap out of it, Vera, it's not the time, get in the car and drive it home, I'll be there after I do what Angel told me to do." Vera did what her mother instructed and cried all the way back home in her mother's car. She didn't want to believe it was her brothers that were dead. She got home and turned on the news to get more information about the story. She stood frozen in front of the TV and a reporter was interviewing an older man and the man was saying, "The young kid that lived here had walked a young lady in a yellow dress to her car."

The older man continued, "I had seen him go back to his apartment then two men dressed in all black walking really fast went up the stairs behind him." Vera thought to herself, *"Yellow dress! Zari, you bitch!"*

Vera called Zari not expecting her to answer her phone but she did and Vera's emotions took over. Vera could feel her heart beating through her chest, she could feel the tension in her muscles and the cracking of her voice as nervousness and anxiety set in. Vera threatened Zari and instantly felt bad about what she just said to her best friend. She ended the call feeling disappointed in herself. She knows Zari well and she didn't really believe Zari had turned on her brothers but she had no one else to blame, no one to take her frustrations and anger out on. Vera's mother was staring at her and asked her skeptically if she really thought Zari had indeed set her brothers up. Not expecting an answer, Vera's mother continued, "You know damn well Zari wouldn't do that to Israel and most importantly, she wouldn't do that to you." Vera lowered her eyes, now staring at the ground as the tears began to flow down her cheek.

Then a knock at the door startled them both. "Who is it?" yelled Vera's mother, as she walked to look into the door peephole. Two zipping noise could be heard and then two holes in the door were exposed. Vera screamed as her mother's body dropped to the floor. She stood up to run and looked at her mother's disfigured bloody face. She screamed again, the door was kicked open and Vera noticed the face of the gunman. *"Yogi Bear,"* she thought to herself as he looked menacing now with a bald head. He asked Vera where was Carla and the bitch, Zari. Vera began walking backwards with her hands held in front of her in a submissive position, crying and saying "please don't kill me, please." "Bitch, where are they at?" Yogi asked, talking through his teeth. Vera tripped over the area rug and fell back on her ass, still moving backward, sliding on her ass across the floor and still pleading for her life. Yogi grew tired of the pleading and emptied his clip into Vera. Vera raised her hands to shield herself from the shower of bullets. She saw the first few flashes from Yogi's gun; she closed her eyes and turned her head away from Yogi. The first bullet hit her in the hand, the second ripped her finger completely off. A few bullets entered her knees and chinbone; bullets ripped through her chest and tore a hole in her jaw. Vera lay on the floor struggling to breathe and she couldn't move. She still felt the bullets piercing her body but she could no longer fight. She felt the blood building up in her mouth. As it began to spill out of her mouth her breathing became more difficult to do. She began taking a slow deep breath. Her breathing slows down and her eyes began to feel like she could only catch glimpses of the broom in the kitchen on the side of the refrigerator. She tried so hard to keep starring at that broom and not close her eyes. She inhaled one last deep breath of air and the broom and kitchen were replaced with blackness. Yogi stood over Vera's now lifeless body and stared at her face and he felt nothing. He understood he was becoming the monster he needed to be in ordered to move forward with life. Yogi bent down to grab Vera's cell phone and looked and seen Zari's number as the last call made. He looked over at a Vera and said, "That's what you get, bitch, and your dumb ass friends are going to get theirs too." He raised his gun and shot Vera one more time in the face. "You ain't so pretty anymore," he said mockingly. He chuckled at what he has just done; he got up and walked out of the door with the least amount of concern for the people he just killed.

PATRICIA and NEVAEH

Patricia sat slightly with her back to the passenger side window so she could look at Nevaeh as she talked so she could see if Nevaeh was lying or not. Patricia repeatedly tapped her finger on the armrest as she stared at her eldest daughter's facial expressions and lip movements. Nevaeh was relaxed and comfortable addressing the questions her mother had. Nevaeh had on a bob wig that was black with blonde highlights, she wore a light blue t-shirt, some fitted jeans, and some blue wedges, her finger, and toenails matched her shoes. For as tough as she is, she loved to dress being a woman and everything that came with being a woman. She loved that guys tried to break their necks to talk to her, to take care of her, and shower her with attention but she also loved the power she felt not needing any of them for anything than what she wanted at that moment. Nevaeh knew her mother was paying attention to her mannerisms, looking for her to do something out of the normal. Patricia had been doing that for years since her sisters and she were little kids. So Nevaeh didn't waste time; she got straight to the point. "Well, Mom, this dude I know from the hood that gets work from me from time to time asked about setting up this kid that plays ball for Whiskey." "WORK?" Patricia said confused. "Drugs, mom." Nevaeh calmly explained the slang before continuing. "He asked me to ask Whiskey for permission to rob one of his basketball players and he would give Whiskey 20% of the money. Whiskey agreed and I taxed another 5% on top of the 20% and then the dude, Angel, asked me to set the young boy up but I didn't know the young boy so Angel asked if Zari could set him up because he had seen her talking to the young boy at the basketball game."

Patricia was staring at Nevaeh with disbelief but didn't say a word. Nevaeh continued, "I offered the deal to Zari to make some easy money since Whiskey sanctioned it, I assumed nothing wrong would happen. "But you were wrong," Patricia interrupted. "Yeah," Nevaeh said before continuing. "All Zari had to do was text Angel when the young kid was alone, the end. She wouldn't even be in the house and she wasn't. They weren't supposed to kill the kid; he made play money for Whiskey, so it should've been an easy robbery but clearly something went wrong. So, I had a meeting with Whiskey and he introduces me to his new right-hand man. Some kid named, "Bear," but the streets say he goes by Yogi." "Yogi Bear," Patricia interrupted again. "I know his mother and it's rumored that Yogi Bear is one of Whiskey's kids." "Oh yeah," Nevaeh replied unfazed by this revelation. Patricia rolled her eyes as she thought to herself. Nevaeh continued, "Well, Whiskey called that morning saying that he wanted everybody in that family dead. So I sent him Angel's address, that's it. I haven't told Zari any of that information because it's handled and she doesn't need to concern herself with that."

Patricia was about to speak and Nevaeh interrupted, "before you tell me, Ma, I know I shouldn't have included Zari but I was trying to help open her eyes to the hustle and have her earn some money for school in the process." Patricia cut Nevaeh off, "You don't know what I'm about to say, hell! It is time for her to learn a few hustles. I'm just upset you didn't give me a heads up. I really don't understand why Whiskey would green-light the robbery of his own worker. He's a selfish, heartless bastard. Listen to me Good, Neveah, he's going to burn you sooner or later, and you better start thinking of an exit plan." Patricia looked around Nevaeh's car and noticed it was clean but old. "Why the fuck are you driving this raggedy-ass car?" Nevaeh replied, "I like to keep a low profile, Ma, and it works for me. I'll get something fancy when I settled down and some man asks me to get married one day." Patricia laughed and joked, "Nobody is marrying your tough ass, you better start looking for women." They both laughed. Patricia asked Neveah to take her home. Neither of them said another word on the ride home, they just listen to Mary J Blige sing to them.

CARLA

Carla stepped out of the shower still wet and walked into her bedroom area and let her feet sink into her plush grey carpet that felt extra comfortable. She noticed the shape of her body in the many mirrors that were the face of her dresser, end tables, and chest. Each bedroom furniture piece was silver with mirrors on the front of each. Each piece also has rhinestones on them. It was a Queen's room and Carla enjoyed being in her room. It was her Oasis. Her light in the middle of the room was a small chandelier to add elegance. Carla laid on a black towel in the center of her bed. She enjoyed air drying this way after a shower or bath. She laid on her back feeling the weight of her breast. She thought about Yogi and how she had a better night than she expected. Getting fucked was not a part of her plans but she was happy it turned out the way it did. She reached into the top drawer of her end table and grabbed a pre-rolled joint; she laid back on her bed, lit the joint and took a hit. She closed her eyes and thought to herself, *"Man, I may have finally found the right man to settle down with, no more fuck boys and pretenders acting like they're bigger than they really are."*

Carla replayed the way Yogi's Hands felt on her body in her mind. She rubbed her hands against her breast, pinching her nipples, her thoughts of Yogi had her aroused but her thoughts were interrupted by her mother yelling her name, "CARLA, Carla, turn on the news. Ain't that the apartments you told me you were going to party at last night?" Carla sat up on the edge of the bed; she cut the TV on with the remote controller to the local news and starred at the screen, still smoking the joint she held. Her eyes grew large as the reporter stated that four men were killed at the apartment complex. Carla made the assumption that Yogi was one of the dead. Carla began to get emotional and laid back on her bed. Although she was sad, no tears would form in her eyes. She shook her head and took another hit of the joint. Then it hit her, "Oh shit, Zari," Carla began calling Zari like crazy to ensure her best friend was good. Carla called Zari until Zari answered. Until the next morning Carla hadn't been sleeping at all. Zari finally answered and Carla began talking fast and loudly, her heart was racing, she was happy to hear her friend's voice but wanted to know what happened. Zari was talking real faint and low. Carla could barely hear her. She asked a few questions and she notices Zari's hesitation to answer questions which wasn't like her. Zari rushed to get off the phone with Carla, this frustrated Carla, and she had been calling all night and morning just for Zari to brush her off the phone. Carla hung the phone up, thinking to herself, *"I know this bitch knows what the fuck happened, I just don't know why she's not telling me."* Carla laid back on her bed, still upset at how the call went. She closed her eyes for a second and sleep took over.

Carla was awakened by her mother the next afternoon. Carla was still naked lying on the towel. "Baby, wake up, something bad happened to one of your friends." Carla's mother said out of breath. Carla slowly woke up as her mother covered her with another towel. "What time is it, ma?" Carla asked. "It's the afternoon," Carla's mother replied not really answering the question. "Something happened to the sweet, pretty little Hispanic girl you and Zari hang around with. It's on the news," she continued. Carla sat up not sure she could handle any more disappointment. Carla was disappointed about Yogi possibly being dead but she didn't think she could handle something happening to one of her girls. She knew her mother was talking about Vera. Carla only hung out with Zari and Vera. She trembled as she turned on her TV.

The News reporter was talking in front of Vera's House, Yellow crime scene tape blocked off the onlookers and the other new reporters. Carla could barely hear the reporter, she only heard the words a mother and daughter found dead and believe to be linked to the deaths at the apartment complex; shooting reported the other night.

Carla's mind began to race and she struggled, trying to piece together everything she was hearing. She looked at her phone and knew she needs to call Zari and find out what the fuck happened and find out who would've wanted to kill Vera and her mother and how was this linked to little Kobe's party which Vera didn't attend. Carla began to wonder if she needed to worry about protecting herself. She began to cry and her mother hugged her and held on to Carla. Carla's mother began to rock her like she was a baby.

Carla was an only child and was spoiled beyond comprehension. Carla took full advantage of her mother's love for her. Carla planned at that moment that she would go over to Zari's house to talk to her face to face. Zari wasn't good at lying and Carla knew Zari wasn't good at confrontation as well. Carla planned to apply pressure on Zari and force her to answer her questions. Carla stood up from her mother and told her she was going to drive over to Zari's and make sure she was okay. Carla's mother agreed that would be a good idea. She gave Carla a couple of hundred dollars for her to take Zari out so they couldn't have their alone time with each other.

See, the thing is, Carla did have guys that loved her and that would take care of her but the bulk of her money and material items she got came from her mother. That persona of the super player that gets money out of every dude she meets was just an illusion. She was being bankrolled and funded by her mother. Carla got dressed quickly and was grabbing her mother's keys to leave to go to Zari's when she looked down at her phone because it began to vibrate and she checked the phone caller ID and she paused and could not talk after seeing the name "Yogi Bear" appeared on the screen.

TIA

Tia was awakened to the smells of bacon, she slowly stretched, balling her fist and reaching above her head. She curled in a ball and pointed her toes to the end of the bed as she exhaled air. She reached over to the end table and grabbed her phone to check to see if Israel had texted or called. He hadn't and she instantly wanted to cry but was interrupted by the sound of laughter from her baby boy. The sound brought a smile to her face and she hurried out of bed and rushed to the living room area to see the face that brought her so much joy. Tia noticed her son in his diapers and socks with no shirt on, holding on to the edge of his grandmother's living room table. He would let go of the edge of the table and flop down on his butt and burst into laughter. Tia's mother, who had on a long nightgown with daisy flowers all over it and her hair pulled back into a ponytail, watched the news and slowly sipped tea out of a large red cup with the words "bitch try me" on the front of it. "Hey, Ma," Tia said while smiling at her son. "How are you feeling this morning?" Tia's mother responded, "I'm fine, just watching this sad shit on the news about some young people being killed last night." Tia raised her eyebrow and inhaled deeply, while never looking up at the TV screen. "It's the hood, ma, these type of things happens all the time," Tia said unfazed. "Yeah, that's true and that's the problem," Tia's mother said. She continued, "Those people were somebody's sons, daughters, fathers or mothers. Four people lost their lives and we as a people just don't care," She said with disappointment and hopelessness in her voice. Tia shrugged her shoulders and continued watching her son play. "I bet you would feel differently if 10 to 12 years from now that Israel Jr. or someone you loved died and the story is on the news," she continued. Tia looked at her mom and rolled her eyes. "Why would you even say something like that?" Tia snapped. Tia's mom responded, "You're proving my point."

Tia got up from the floor and walked into the kitchen to eat the breakfast that woke her out of her sleep. She checked her phone and had a text from her friend Nakala about coming to the bar so she can learn the ropes and start making money. Tia smiled and sat down to eat at the dining room table. Tia started thinking about what her mother had said and how she would feel if it was her son or Israel. She quickly changed her thought and started thinking that she was going to hug Israel and put an end to their beef by fucking him like she never had before. Israel had wanted her to swallow when she gives him head and she never would. She knew she needed to make up with him but also sell him on the idea that she was about to work in the strip club. Nakala told her to wear a black t-shirt and some black boycott shorts, black boots with black leggings. Tia needed to go to the mall and buy the black shorts and leggings. She figured she would swing by Israel's house on the way back from the mall to give him the best head he ever had and finish the job by swallowing. She smiled at the thought and finished her breakfast. She thought about putting on her favorite jeans that made her ass looked the best. She was going to wear a white t-shirt with no bra so her pierced nipples would show through her shirt the way Israel liked. She was going to make sure her lip gloss was extra wet looking for him. She knew to wear her red panties because red was Israel's favorite color. Her thoughts were broken when her son came into the dining room scooting with the TV remote controller in hand. He was crawling on one knee with a huge smile on his face as his grandmother's voice was heard yelling, "Bring me back that damn remote, little crazy boy." Tia laughed at what her son was putting her mom through.

Tia asked her mother if she could borrow her car. Tia's mother said yes without hesitation, she was filled with joy to have her only daughter and grandson in the home with her because they brought so much life into the home. She had been lonely since retiring from her job one year prior. "I hope you're going to see about a job?" she said jokingly, never looking up from the television. "Yes, ma'am," Tia responded proudly. "I already have the job; I just need to get the items to wear to work," Tia continued. They both smiled at each other and Tia went and got dressed to head to the Mall. Tia was getting urges to stop by Israel's place before she went to the mall but decided she better stay on point and stick to her plan. She decided a drive-by wouldn't hurt. Tia drove by the house and she noticed Israel's brother and cousin weren't outside and that the front door was closed, which was unusual. Tia blew off the oddness of how dead the house looked. She noticed a really nice Mercedes Benz on the street and told herself that she would get a car like that if she hustles hard and stayed focused. Tia continued on to the mall and got the items she was looking for and head back to Israel's house. She started getting excited thinking about seeing her man.

She was so excited she was leaning all over the steering wheel, sitting as close as she could to it. She took a deep breath and let out a "whoa" and turned unto Israel's street and as she drove closer to the house she noticed the large crowd of people. She couldn't drive to the house; there were so many people out. She pulled over, parked, and began walking toward the house. She noticed the news channel crews and all the police cars. She heard the news reporter talking about Israel's home like they knew who lived there and her heart began to race. She began to lose her breathe the closer she got to the house. She began fighting through the crowd making her way to the police line. "Oh, my God! Oh, my God! What the fuck!" Tia mumbled to herself. She arrived at the police line and saw the coroners removing a body and Tia lost it and started screaming and ran towards the coroners that were handling the body. Tia wanted to see who it was that was dead. She was pushed back by the police, telling her she needs to get back behind the lines. Tia started screaming that she lived in the house. "She lives here, that's her family." An Old man screamed at the police. A detective ran towards the crowd to see what the ruckus was all about. He heard the young lady screaming, "I live here, I live here!" The detective made his way to her and asked Tia if she said she lived there. Tia was upset and crying. She wanted to know whose body that was and the detective began to ask her another question. The coroners came out with a second body and Tia dropped to her knees and cried who was dead. She whaled out screams and started to feel faint. She kept thinking it was Israel but she tried to not think it was him and her hands began to shake uncontrollably and she cried out, "Lord, no, not Israel."

The detective grabbed her and told her and said, "I can tell you right now that there were two women that were killed here today and if you live here you can help us and identify the bodies and answer some questions for us. I'm detective Judge Carter." Tia was still crying but no longer screaming hysterically. The detective continued, "Just call me Judge."

Detective Judge wanted Tia to look at the bodies to confirm their identities; he told her they could just look at the bodies because their faces were unrecognizable and then she could answer the questions he had so they could get some understanding to who might want to hurt them this way. Tia confirmed some tattoos on Vera and her mother's bodies. She cried as she thought about what this would do to Israel, she knew this would kill him, learning how his mother and baby sister died. She started wondering where Israel and his brother were at. She was thinking did Angel do something that somebody would want to kill his family. She thought about how she and the baby could've easily been in the house and they could have died with them and the thought made her cry some more. Tia turned to the detective who was trying to usher her to his car and she told him she didn't want to go to the police station and she could answer any questions he had now. Tia continued, "I don't know why anyone would want to kill them." Detective Judge asked, "Well, who else lives in the home." Tia was hesitant to answer and Detective Judge continued, "Your neighbors already told us two guys live here as well; I just want to know their names." Tia answered Israel and Angel. "Do you know if they had any issues with anybody?" Detective Judge asked. "No, they didn't have any issues with anyone," Tia responded. Tia couldn't believe what she was saying in her heart she knew this had something to do with Angel.

Detective Judge took out his business card and told Tia he would be in touch with her and to call him if she thought of anything or learned of anything. He nodded his head and turned to walk away. Detective Judge knew Israel and Angel were dead and he planned to pay a visit to Tia in the morning. He wanted to see if she would change her mind by the morning and help piece this puzzle together for him and the other detectives working the case. He was going to get with the other detective that was working on Israel and Angel's robbery-gone wrong case to compare information with his case. He turned and look back at Tia one last time, thinking of how tomorrow would become much worst for her, and walked back into the house to continue studying the crime scene.

Tia turned and looked at the house and coroner's van; tears began to fall from her eyes. She knew she would never come back to that house again. "Where the fuck are you Israel?" she thought to herself walking back to her mom's car. She looked at her phone and still no messages from Israel. She had a few missed calls from her mother. Tia was walking with her head down looking at her phone. She got to her mother's car, open the door, and sat in the driver's seat. She was crying as she texted her mother. "I'll be home in a minute, something terrible happened." She hit send and then attempted to call Israel again. She lifted her head up as the phone rang. She noticed the fancy Mercedes Benz pulling up slowly a little too close to her mom's car, the driver side window started rolling down as it got side by side next to Tia's driver side window. She leaned closer to the window and she squints her eyes to try and see who was driving the car. A silencer on a barrel of a gun became visible and before Tia could react a flash was the last thing Tia saw.

WHISKEY

Whiskey was at his pool hall sitting in his office, rocking back and forth with a glass of whiskey in his hand. His cherry wood desk didn't have anything out of place on it. He rarely actually did anything on the desk other than sit his whiskey drink down on it. He smiled as he talked to Yogi, Whiskey was proud of himself. He thought to himself, *"I've found me a new right-hand man, whom I can control and he just so happened to be one of my kids."* He stared at Yogi, feeling good about being able to leave his business to a family member whom he could mold. Yogi was relaxed leaning back in his chair, he struggled sitting still without anything to do. Whiskey was talking about basketball, reminiscing about Aiden. He was trying to get Yogi to remember the good times he had with Aiden. Yogi didn't smile or laugh at any of the stories, didn't even seem he was listening at all. Whiskey noticed but kept talking anyway because the memories were amusing to him.

Whiskey's cell phone vibrated and he looked at his phone to see if he wanted to take the call or not, it was Neveah. Whiskey still laughing as he answered, Whiskey leaned forward in his chair, "Oh yeah," he said. Whiskey looked at Yogi with a serious sinister look which caused Yogi to set up in his chair. Whiskey said good job and ended the call. He leaned towards Yogi and said, "Remember that fine ass tomboy, Nevaeh, I introduce you to that work for me that you was lusting over." Yogi nodded but remained serious. Whiskey continued, "Well, she got the address for the family of the guys that killed little Kobe." Yogi stood up and his head began to pound as the rage filled his body. Yogi felt the evil taking over his soul. Whiskey knew the look, it was familiar to him, he remembers being filled with the same evil spirit as a teenager when he killed the man that killed his parents and brothers leaving him for dead as well. Whiskey knew a monster when he saw it and Yogi had indeed become a monster. Whiskey handed over the address. Yogi took the paper out of Whiskey's hand and headed to the exit. Whiskey called out to Yogi. "Kill anybody in that motherfucka." Yogi stopped and turned to face Whiskey, "Indeed," Yogi said. Whiskey gave a head nod to Yogi and reached for his drink and Yogi grinded his teeth and left without saying another word.

Whiskey lean back in his chair and took another sip of the whiskey he had been drinking. He figured he would get out of the office and shoot some pool with some of the other old heads that hung out at the pool hall all day reminiscing about their youth and talking shit about who had the most money and who had the sexist woman and who still was in the best shape currently. Whiskey enjoyed these moments because it allowed him to forget he was a monster, it allowed him to forget all the hard decisions he had to make. Activities like gambling on basketball allowed him to escape his own insanity. These are the times he felt normal. A few hours had passed and Whiskey was shooting pool and laughing with four other gentlemen when the breaking new story took over the TV screens. "Two women found shot to death and the police have no leads," the news reporter said. Whiskey smiled about his boy and the work he have been putting in. *"That boy the truth,"* whiskey thought to himself. He went back to playing pool and talking shit with the group of guys. A half of day had passed and Whiskey began to get tired and had planned on going to one of his houses and lay up and watch movies and have dinner with a young woman. Whiskey said his goodbyes to some people in his organization that were sitting at the bar drinking and he headed to his Corvette. He got to his car door and heard someone call his name. Whiskey turned and smiled, which turned into a laugh. Before Whiskey could gather his composure from laughing, two shots rang out, knocking Whiskey backwards into his car door. He began sliding down his car door to the ground as he tried to look into the eyes of his assailant. "Mothafucka" was all he heard as the person disappeared into the night and people from the pool hall came out running to help him.

YOGI

Yogi got in the Benz as fast as he could. He wanted to kill anybody related to the niggas that killed his brother. Yogi was biting down on his bottom lip so hard that it began to bleed. The blood began to run down his chin but he didn't even notice. He was getting locked in for what he had to do. He stopped at a red light when noticed his mother at a gas station getting gas. Yogi had not dealt with his mother much since Aiden was killed and he pulled over into the gas station to speak with her before the son she knew and raised was lost forever to the monster he was becoming. He wiped the blood off his face and pulled in behind his mother's car. He startled his mother; she paused and reached into her coat jacket. Yogi spoke, "Hey, ma". She relaxed as she noticed Yogi's face. He looked different to her, his innocence was gone. His face was hardened, gone was the child-like presences he had always had. Yogi broke his mother's thoughts when he laughed and asked her "What are you reaching for, Ma?" She chuckled and said, "You better ask around about me. I'll put hot lead in somebody ass." They both laughed as Yogi reached out and hugged his mother. She was happy to see Yogi. She asked him why haven't he been around to see her, and told him she was really worried about him. Yogi responded, "Mom, I'm fine, I just been hanging out with Whiskey, and he's helping me deal with the death of Aiden." She retorted, "That man is pure evil and he will be the death of us all." Yogi responded, "It's cool, mom, I know how to handle myself and I just wanted to say hi and hug your neck. I got somewhere to be." Yogi's mom responded, "Let me guess, you got to take care of something for Whiskey. He probably got you selling dope or worst." Yogi stopped his mom. "Nobody got me doing anything; I'm my own man doing what needs to be done," Yogi said to his mother aggressively. She stared at her son in shock. Yogi never talked to his mother that way. She paused, "Okay, baby, I love you but when you're in jail remember who got you there." Yogi hugged his mother and kissed her on her forehead, "No, one is going to jail, ma." Yogi broke his embrace and got back into his car. He stared at his mother as she got into her car, he knew his mother would need to learn to love the person he was becoming or lose him forever. Yogi's mother got into her car and realized she was losing her son, "Damn, you Whiskey." She pulled out of the gas station with tears starting to flow from her eyes.

Yogi had to refocus after seeing his mother, so he pictured Aiden's body folded over on itself lifeless. The anger rushed back into his mind, he rushed to the address to finish his mission. Yogi got to the street and drove to the address listed on the paper. The street was empty; Yogi parked several houses down and watched the house for a few moments. He could no longer wait. He was supposed to make sure no extra people were in the house first but the anger was too much. Yogi put the silencer on the gun to suppress the sound of the gun shots. Yogi got to the door and decided, "I'm shooting everybody in this ugly ass house." Yogi knocked on the door and waited to hear a voice. "Who is it?" a raspy voice lady yelled. The voice irritated Yogi, as soon as he heard the voice again; he fired a shot and decided to fire another to ensure the first body fell. Yogi looked at the woman's face exploded and then her body dropped to the ground. Yogi mumbled, "Yeah, bitch." A scream to his right broke him out of his trance and he focused his attention on the person screaming. *"That's the bitch that was with Carla and Zari,"* Yogi thought. Without thinking he asked Vera where the fuck is Carla and that bitch, Zari. Yogi saw the fear and shock in Vera's eyes and he knew it was pointless to talk to her and he decided to empty his clip. Yogi could see her brother's face in hers and he wanted to shoot it off. Yogi wanted to fuck up her pretty face and as he got ready to pull the trigger, Vera fell and yogi missed the first shot and hit the wall. Vera slid across the floor with her hands up pleading and begging for her life. Yogi felt power; he felt Vera giving all her energy and power to him at that moment. He fired a flurry of shots at her face. Yogi imagined it was Israel that he was shooting. Vera lay on the floor heavily breathing, Yogi stood over her as she took her last breath. Yogi searched Vera's body and took her phone. He noticed Zari's phone number and got excited at the thought of killing her. Yogi fired another shot into Vera's face for good measure. He knew he was talking but he didn't even remember what he was saying. Yogi was having an out of body experience. Yogi was losing himself to Bear. Bear chuckled at the *mayhem* he just created and Yogi was no longer.

Bear got back in his car and sat there. He put the car in drive to leave but he wanted to see the aftermath of what he did. Just like when he wanted to see the aftermath when he shot that tall guy that owed Whiskey money. Bear had now killed or shot few people and he was enjoying it. A crowd of people began to come out of their homes and before Bear could pull off, a fire truck followed by an ambulance showed up on the scene. The police arrived a few minutes later. Bear wasn't nervous about being on the scene he was prepared to shoot it out with the police and die if necessary. He enjoyed the energy he was feeling, the fear, the sorrow, and the concern of the neighbors. The fire department left the scene and the police began taping off the crime scene. A large crowd gathered looking on. An old man looked at Bear as he walked past the car. Bear let the window down flashing his gun. "You see something, old man?" he said staring the old man down. The Gun startled the old man,"Naw, I ain't seen shit." and kept walking towards the crowd. Bear smirked at the old man's response. Bear thought to himself that he had seen enough and was ready to pull off when he noticed Israel's baby momma walking towards the scene. "It must be my lucky day," Bear said. "I remember her from school, that bitch can get it too, he continued, "I'm sending anybody that fuck with that nigga to meet his ass." Bear was grinding his teeth and mumbling to himself. He watched her go to the scene and start crying and screaming. He watched the bodies brought out, he watched her talk to a detective. He watched her walk right past his car with her head down texting. He started his car as she got in hers; he pulled right up to her window. He glanced at her and when she lifted her head, he realized how beautiful she was but fired a single shot into her forehead. *"What a waste!"* he thought. The glass shattered and caused some people to look towards the cars but Bear kept driving laughing out loud to himself. Bear drove back to his old neighborhood and pulled into the parking lot of the apartment he shared with his brother, Aiden. Bear knew at some point the police would come looking for him being a dead man's roommate and Whiskey was going to help him with an alibi for his whereabouts on the night of the murder. Bear wanted to go into the apartment so bad but he also knew being in there would weaken him. Yogi took out Vera's phone and manually transferred Zari's contact into his burner phone. And he searched for Carla's number and did the same for her contact information. He read through Vera's text messages and read messages from Angel to Vera asking if Zari would go through with the robbery or not. That's all Bear needed to confirm that Zari was indeed involved and enough for him to condemn Carla as well. They both were going to pay for their involvement.

Bear figures he would get something to eat to get his energy back up and pay Carla a visit. Bear went to the same taco spot him and Carla went on their first night together, he wanted to remember that night. There was a small part of him that wished things were different, Bear shook the thought off and called Carla. Carla answered on the first ring, which caught Bear off guard. "YOGI, Yogi, oh my God, Yogi is this you for real." Her excitement was stunning. Bear didn't know if she was really this excited or she was a really good actor. "Omg baby, I thought you were dead. Where are you at baby, I'm coming to you right now!" Carla said in an electrified voice. Bear still didn't know how to respond. He wasn't expecting this energy from her. "I'm just riding, we can meet up," Bear said. Carla responded, "Okay, I was on my way to see Zari to try and find out what the fuck happen but I'll see her later, I want to see you right now. What the fuck happened Yogi?" Carla asked. Yogi was confused; he started believing that Carla honestly didn't know anything. Yogi thought to himself that he needed to look her in the eyes to see if she was lying or not. He gave her the address to one of the apartment buildings Whiskey owned. Carla said she would be there in twenty minutes and hung up. Bear took the sim card of Vera's phone and broke it in half and then threw it out the window. He headed to meet Carla with mixed emotions.

Carla was waiting for Yogi when he pulled up. She got out of the car and got into the passenger side of the car. She looked at Yogi and hugged and kissed him hard. "Damn, don't do that to me, man. I've been crying all night, I thought you were dead. Vera's dead and I don't know what the fuck is going on. Zari ain't saying shit. What the fuck happened?" Carla asked concerned. Bear could see the sincerity in her eyes and mannerism. Bear began to explain what happen but Bear still had his gun between his legs in case she slipped up. "Well, after I dropped you off, I went back to the apartment and finished the tacos in the parking lot. I fell asleep and I woke up when somebody bumped the car and before I realized that niggas were trying to rob Aiden." Bear's jaws got tight and he began to talk in a deeper lower tone. Carla rubbed his arm, "Baby, it's okay," she said. Carla noticed for the first time how different Yogi looked, how his arms felt different. She let go of her thoughts and continued listening. Bear continued, "By the time I got up the stairs they had killed him already. I failed my brother, pretending to be tough and I wasn't built for any gangster shit.

Well, I'm built for it now. I killed all three of those muthafuckas as they came out of the apartment. And here is where it gets crazy," Yogi continued, "The three niggas were your homegirl Vera's family, her brother Angel, Israel, and their cousin." "What the fuck?" Carla said covering her mouth with her hands. Bear continued, "Carla, your friends set Aiden up." Carla dropped her hand to her lap and leaned back against the passenger door, "Naw man, no," she mumbled. Bear continued with the story, "Vera knew about it and Zari was in on it too." "Ain't no fucking way Zari could do something like that!," Carla yelled, "Aint no fucking way." Bear continued, "I read the text messages that Angel sent Vera making sure Zari would go through with it. I killed Vera, her mother, and Israel's kid mother too for being related to that hoe ass nigga." Carla was speechless. After a few moments of silence, Carla repeated, "Yogi, you killed Vera?" "Yes, I did, and I'm going to kill Zari too. You're going to have to pick a side now." Tears formed and began to run down Carla's face. "What you mean you're going to kill Zari, it has to be a mistake," Carla said still crying. Bear asked again, "Pick your side between me and her because she has to die for what she did." Carla was crying, in total disbelief of what was happening as she was shaking her head no and covering her face with her hands. Carla lifted her head and told Yogi that she couldn't do it. She couldn't knowingly live with the fact she let her best friend get killed. She dropped her head back down, crying and using her hand to wipe away tears from her face.

Four shots rang out hitting Carla in the chest. Carla was thrown backward by the shots. She looked at Yogi confused and trying to catch her breath. She struggled to say Yogi's name as she began to cough up blood. "It's Bear Beautiful," Bear said with regret in his tone. Carla tried to reach out to Yogi and he knocked her hands away. "I didn't shoot you in the face so you could have a proper funeral, babygirl." Bear said to a dying Carla not breaking eye contact with her. Bear reached for Carla's phone, he broke the phone in half and waited for Carla to stop fighting and pass into the unknown. Carla's eyes began to roll in her head and her breathing became harder and harder to complete. Carla's head slumped and she exhaled her last breath. Bear stared at Carla for a few moments, "Damn, babygirl, I'm glad to know you didn't have anything to do with

Aiden's death but I had to kill you, I couldn't risk you fucking everything up." Bear leaned over and open the passenger's door of the car and pushed Carla's dead body out of the car and Headed to Zari's house so he can finish what they started.

ZARI

Zari's sleep was disturbed by Hazel. Hazel had a joint in her hand and a glass of cranberry and vodka. "Here Zari take a hit of this and drink this vodka." Zari wiped her eyes with her hand. She was disoriented but she reached for the joint and took a puff. She took a sip of the drink and passed it back to her sister. Hazel began talking while staring at her younger sister, jazzy rhythm and blues type music played on her phone. "You cried yourself to sleep, baby girl, you got yourself into some bullshit, didn't you." "But, Nevaeh..."Zari began to talk; Hazel interrupted her, "But Navaeh, my ass, you're a grown-ass woman, Zari, you need to do what's best for you. We were all raised in this same house, witnessing and learning the same bullshit evils Patricia allowed us to be engulfed in. We all rough around the edges and maybe we all bend the rules some but Neveah and Patricia were the only ones doing the fuck shit and now you're a part of it. Clearly, you're not strong enough not to get influenced by the evil that resides with us in the house. Look at Capri, she's working to get out of here; she's going be a famous singer better believe it, Nakala working her ass off at night bartending and going to school during the day for nursing, just like you. I'm going to teach and settled down with one of these fine-ass kings soon and build my piece of heaven on earth. Patricia and Nevaeh love the bullshit and lies of the streets. It's a losing game though Zari, look how many people were affected by your one decision." Nevaeh entered the room. "Save all that preachy shit Hazel; your Hippie ass won't ever leave the nest, your ass afraid of any kind of commitment," Nevaeh said rudely. "Zari, we made some food and you need to eat something, we all hanging out on the porch. You need to get out of this room and be around your family and Hazel, bring your ass too," Nevaeh said, giving Hazel the side-eye.

Zari wanted to shower first. She told Nevaeh that she would be there after she showered. Nevaeh gave her a head nod and left the room.

Hazel got up off Zari's bed and rubbed Zari's shoulder and followed behind Nevaeh. Zari let the shower water run down her face, she combed her finger through her hair with her eyes close with her face pointing up at the ceiling. The hot water was almost unbearable but that was the way she liked it. Zari wanted to believe the water was washing away her sins as it ran over her body. She began to cry uncontrollably and mumbled a prayer asking for forgiveness and praying the nightmare would end and praying that she could take it all back. Patricia knocked on the door and asked Zari if she was alright. Stopping her prayer, "Yeah, mom, I'm good," Zari responded feeling everything but good. Zari cut the water off and stood in the tub looking at the water running down and falling off her body. Patricia continued, "Alright, I just wanted to check on you." "Okay, mama, I'll be out in a minute," Zari responded. "Okay baby," Patricia said walking away from the door. Zari was still standing in the tub; she took a deep breath and stepped out of the shower. She walked to the mirror and wiped the stream from the mirror to see her face. She wanted to make sure her eyes weren't puffy from crying. She stared at herself in the mirror thinking about Vera and Aiden and how she doomed herself to hell. She began to tell herself she has to dedicate her life to saving lives to make up for the lives that were lost. She stared in the mirror, disgusted with the person she saw looking back at her. She wrapped herself in a towel and headed to her room to get dressed. Zari decided some jeans, flip-flops and a white tee would do. Her hair was still wet some and she didn't really care. She didn't have an Appetite but figured she better do what her sister, Nevaeh, requested. Zari walked into the kitchen to see a spread of food on the dining room table. It was like it was the fourth of July. It was BBQ ribs, grilled hot dogs, baked beans, cheese-stuffed hamburgers, potato salad, and mac and cheese. Zari grabbed a plate, put some mac and cheese on the plate and warmed it up in the microwave, and stepped on the porch. To Zari's surprise, her mom and all her sisters were on the porch eating food and laughing, listening to music despite her sadness, seeing her family together all at one time put a smile on her face. Nakala saw and spoke to Zari first. "Hey, girly, glad you can join us," and she smiled at Zari. Patricia reached for Zari's hand and grabbed it just wanting to support her baby girl. Hazel and Capri were singing the music and dancing, Nevaeh was standing at the bottom stair, looking really girly with her hair pressed and hanging down to her shoulders. She was wearing a pink t-shirt, jeans, and pink and gray Nike air max shoes.

Zari was smiling at Nevaeh and how cute she was with her hair down. When out of the corner of her eye, a figure entered her view and causing a discerned look on her face. It was a man pointing a gun at her. She gasped and shots began to ring out. Bullets pierced her body as she fell backward grabbing Nakala as she fell and they both fell to the ground. Patricia screamed as she dropped her plates and dove on to the porch ground, trying to shield her daughters from being shot. Hazel grabbed Capri and jumped on top of her to shield her from the shots. The gunman was still firing shots at Zari and walking towards the porch. Nevaeh reached for her gun with pure horror expressed on her face as she saw her baby sister get shot. She tried to return fire before getting struck in the shoulder and her hip. She looked at the shooter and screamed, "Wait, wait, what are you doing? It was approved by Whiskey."

BEAR

Bear felt a small sense of sadness as he thought about killing Carla. He was excited to get to Zari's house and kill her. Bear figured he would ride past the house and study to find out who were all at her house as he turned on the street. He noticed a group of ladies on the porch of the house. He was shocked to see the pretty tomboy that Whiskey introduced him to there. "What the fuck she is doing here?" He thought as he pulled over one house over but across the street from Zari's home. One of the ladies looked in his direction but looked away. Bear noticed how they all looked similar but he didn't see Zari. Bear sat there confused trying to put it together. Bear was sitting there trying to figure out the relationship between Zari and the pretty tomboy and why did she give information on Israel's family if she knew her people or friends were in on the robbery. He tried to focus and weigh his options and how he was going to kill Zari. When she stepped out of the house and stood on the porch. The sight of her curly hair and her smiling infuriated him so much that he dropped the potential plan he was trying to come up with and got out of the car and headed to the porch without thinking.

Bear could see her smiling and having a good time while his brother was dead. *This bitch is up there having a good time and I'm left with nothing but pain*, Bear thought to himself as he pointed his gun at her. He got to the sidewalk when she noticed him, Bear wanted to wipe that smile off her face and he opened fire. Bear enjoyed seeing her white shirt turn bloody and he enjoyed seeing her body fall to the ground. He kept firing; he didn't care if the other women were getting in the way, they could die too. He thought to himself. Bear noticed the pretty tomboy reaching for her gun and he fired a few shots at her dropping her to one knee. She started screaming, "wait, wait, what are you doing, with her palms of her left hand raised facing him trying to make a shield from the gunshots, "Whiskey approved it." The statement paused Bear for a second. He stared at Nevaeh and responded, "Then he needs to die too," and fired a single shot into her forehead and her body fell forward on the bottom step of the porch. Bear turned his attention back to Zari and imagined shooting her in the face until she was no longer pretty. As he took a few steps toward the porch and a neighbor came from the house to the left of Zari's home and return fire at Bear, striking him in the side. Bear clutched his side in pain and turned and run back to his car. He returned shots towards the neighbor and the man took cover. Bear limped back to the car disappointed he couldn't confirm if Zari was dead but drove off in his car headed to Whiskey's.

Bear got to Whiskey's house and noticed a bunch of cars at his house. Bear had to park down the street a few houses and walked back to Whiskey house. He was bleeding and limped his way to the side door and let himself in. Bear was grimacing in pain as he entered the kitchen. There was a chubby woman in the kitchen cooking food. She turned around and saw the blood and yelled to the front of the house. "Whiskey, your boy in here bleeding and shit. Like father, like son." And she turned back around and continued cooking. A few of Whiskey's soldiers came in the kitchen to assist Bear to the living room where Whiskey was laying down on the couch with no shirt on with wraps and bandages on his upper body and a bandage on his face. Whiskey turned to try and see Bear but the gunshot wounds restricted him from doing so. Bear limped to the front of the couch so Whiskey could see him. "Are you alright?" whiskey asked. "I'm alive," Bear replied. Whiskey waived to a tall black man sitting in the corner. "Hey Doc, can you see about my son? I'll pay three times the normal fee." The doctor helped Bear to a room in the back of the house and performed the removal of the bullet. Bear laid on the bed and closed his eyes while the doctor did his work. Bear was disappointed he didn't get a chance to shoot Zari in the face. He thought about Carla and how that could've been something. He thought about how he lost control of Zari's situation and he needs to get that in check. He thought about the last words of Nevaeh and knew he needed to have a conversation with Whiskey. He started thinking he may have to kill Whiskey and how he would do it. Bear thought it was weird hearing Whiskey calling him his son out loud and how the woman in the kitchen seems to know as well. The doctor interrupted Bear's thoughts. "Alright son, you're all done." Bear sat up in pain and went back to the living room and lean back in a lazy boy chair. One of Whiskey's soldiers paid the doctor and the doctor left without saying a word. The chubby woman brought them both plates of food and she looked at Bear up and down but didn't say anything. She turned to Whiskey and said I'll be back in the morning to cook y'all breakfast and clean up around here. Whiskey acknowledged her and said thank you. She looked Bear over again and left out. Whiskey told his soldiers that they're good for the night and that they could go home. "Are you sure boss?" One of the guys asked. "Yeah, I'm sure," whiskey responded. The guy said okay and they turned and left.

Bear could sense that Whiskey was about to say something and he became anxious to get the conversation started. "What happened to you?" Bear asked. Whiskey chuckled and shook his head. "Well, I was heading to my car leaving the pool hall and your mama shot me." "What?" Bear said surprised. Whiskey continued, "Yeah, your mama shot me, she was upset that you are here with me and I guess she wanted to make sure it didn't stay that way. I thought about killing her, I did. I can't lie to you but then I knew I would have to kill you too and I just couldn't do that, you're my blood, you're my son, my family. It's rumored that I fathered all these kids and hell maybe I did, but if I did, their mothers made sure I wasn't a part of y'all lives but here it is, a bad decision lead you to me and I can die peacefully knowing I'm leaving behind everything I built to my own blood. So because of that, I'll give your mother a pass just like I'm hoping you give me one. I have something else to tell you." Bear got nervous and couldn't sit still in his chair anticipating what Whiskey was about to say. Whiskey continued, "I gave the okay for Aiden to be robbed. It's an old hustle I would do every now and then to ensure a player would have to keep playing for me. Nevaeh came to me and said a guy was asking for approval to rob Aiden and I gave the okay. No one was supposed to die and Aiden would lose a few dollars and would still need to play for me but it went wrong and I'm sorry. That's why I made it my priority to have his family killed to seek revenge for what they did. Now I know this is upsetting and you may hate me and want to kill me for giving the approval for the robbery but as your father, I'm asking you for a pass. I'm admitting to you as a man and as your father for you to forgive me and let me die an old man so I can pass my empire to you the way a King is supposed to pass his kingdom to his son. I know your mother didn't tell you and I honored her wishes and stayed away but you're here now and there are very few things I wouldn't do for you. Can you forgive me?" Whiskey asked. Bear just took in all the information before answering. The silence was nerve racking because he didn't know if he should kill Whiskey or be happy about the open acknowledgment about being his father. Bear broke the silence, I learned you were my father the first night I got here, and honestly, I was upset with my mother for not telling me. I felt my life could've been so different and I can't lie I feel some sort of happiness knowing who my father is because I had always been hoping to learn who my father was. Now about my mother, I'm glad you didn't kill her, I'm happy you gave her a pass and I can't lie, I found out you gave the okay about the robbery from the pretty tomboy chick that works for you. "Nevaeh?" Whiskey said. "Yeah, she is dead now so you going to have to replace her." "Damn, I liked her," Whiskey said shaking his head. Bear continued, "I planned on killing you when I got here but all those people were here, and then I thought about it once they all left but honestly I enjoyed the feeling when that fat lady referred to me as your son and you referring to me as the same. Aiden was my brother the only person that made me feel like I mattered. It'll be hard letting him go. I just need to make sure the Zari bitch is dead and I'll move on." "So you forgive me?" Whiskey asked. "Yeah, I forgive you but you have to make up for the lost time." "Thank you, son, you'll get everything and more."

ZARI

Zari woke up from her surgery confused about her whereabouts, her body was sore. She still was heavily medicated and she couldn't focus for long periods of time. Her chest was sore she reached to feel her chest and felt the staples from the middle of her breast down to her navel. She began to cry but it hurt when her body moved. Nakala popped up out of the chair near the window in Zari's room. "Zari, Hey sister, I'm so happy you're awake." Zari asked Nakala what happened. "Some random ass dude walked up in front of the house and shot us." Nakala still had a frightened disbelief facial expression as she told Zari what happened to them. Zari noticed that Nakala's arm was in a case. Nakala looked down at her arm and she noticed Zari looking at it. "Yeah, I got hit in the arm a few times but you pulling me down and mama jumping on us saved our lives probably." "Where's mama?" Zari asked.

"Mama took shots to her back, she's alive but she's going be in a wheelchair, she paralyzed from the waist down. Hazel and Capri are there with her now. She's okay; you know our mother is tough. She did tell us that once you and she get out of the hospital, we're moving immediately to another state. She also said don't tell the police anything, we're just getting out of here and never coming back." Zari was trying to fight back tears, thinking about her mom. Zari was trying to remember what happened. She could only remember seeing the flashes from the gun. She closed her eyes and asked about Nevaeh. Nakala began to cry and she couldn't even say the words. She rubbed the back of her head and neck with her hand; she stared at the ground unable to look Zari in the eyes. "Nevaeh was killed." Zari began to cry uncontrollably and it hurt her body as she cried but she couldn't control it. Nakala just rubbed Zari's head and face gently telling her we'll get through this together and we'll start over when you get out of the hospital. Zari closed her eyes and tried to pray away her regrets.

BEAR

The weather was perfect, kids were running around the neighborhood playing, some neighbors were out grilling BBQ and music was playing and it was a perfect summer day. Some cars blew their horns and waved at Bear as they passed him. He gave a head nod and waved the peace sign in return. Bear was the man now. Bear was at the house of one of his girlfriends. He was getting groceries out of the back of his girlfriend's Yukon Denali. It had been thirteen years since he killed the people involved in Aiden's death. Bear now had a full beard that had gray hair mixed in giving him the salt and pepper look. He worked out a lot and his face was still hardened and he was still in shape. He was now in charge of Whiskey's organization. He also expanded the organization by starting a tech company that developed apps, He restored abandoned buildings and turned them into overnight shelters for people to sleep in for ten dollars a night. He owned a few car dealerships and rented the used car out to people to drive for Uber and Lyft.

Whiskey had passed away two years after being shot by Bear's mother. Whiskey's body couldn't recover from the gunshots and he passed away from low oxygen caused by pneumothorax. Bear had let the thought of killing Zari go. He heard she lived but she and her family moved out of town never to be heard of again. Bear loved his new life, everybody respected him and the rest feared him. The police was on his payroll and he was a God in his own mind. Bear grabbed the groceries out of the trunk and carried them inside of the house and he came back out to grab the bottled waters when he noticed his girlfriend's son and some other kids kicking and beating one kid in the middle of the street. Bear laughed to himself and watched for a little bit at first but figured he needed to break it up so the vibe could stay chill on the block. He put the water on the porch still looking at the kids beating one kid.

He began walking towards the kids and he waited until he got right up on the boys and he didn't say anything but the boys all stopped when they noticed him. "Did he deserve it?" Bear asked the group of boys. "Hell yeah, he doesn't have any business around here," one of the boys responded. "Oh, y'all some type a gang or something?" Bear asked. "Nope!" his girlfriend's kid said quickly. Bear just stared at him without saying a word and turned back to the others boys and asked what he did. "He was talking wreckless about you and the people that work for you," responded one of the kids that had long locs. Bear looked at the boy on the ground, "You know me, little homie?" Bear asked the boy. The Beaten boy sat up and responded, "Yeah, I know who you are." Bear extended his hand to help the boy off the ground. The boy took his hand and Bear used his strength to pull him up. The boy pulled out a gun and pointed it at Bear and without hesitation he fired his weapon. Bear didn't get a chance to react before the bullet entered his forehead and his body fell to the ground. The group of boys started running and Bear's girlfriend kid was screaming, "Izzy just shot Bear!"

IZZY

Izzy grew up with his grandmother and she took good care of him and she did everything she could to shelter him from the streets and any trouble from the neighborhood. Izzy was six foot three inches tall and slim and about to enter his second year of high school. Although his grandmother tried her best, she was older and Izzy would sneak out at night and hang with guys in the streets. He did some robberies and even sold some drugs here and there to buy things he knew his grandmother wouldn't get him. He got himself a gun just to be prepared for whatever may happen. Izzy had heard all the stories about his parents, how they died, and who killed them. It was a bitter subject for him. It causes him great pain. The only family he had was his grandmother and he just never spoke about it until one day playing basketball at the park. This kid was talking about how his mama and Bear were dating and how Bear buys them whatever they wanted. Izzy's heart started pounding; he's just listening to the kid talk so proudly and without a care in the world sparked something in Izzy that hadn't really been ignited before. He wasn't sad, which was the normal, he was mad. He just wanted to shut the nigga up. He was tired of his mouth and hearing about the nigga everybody says killed his parents. "Fuck that nigga and fuck you too!" Izzy just blurted out. When he realized what he said the kid and his friends had already started beating him. Some older guys broke up the fight and Izzy grabbed his gym bag and acted like he left the park but he hid and waited to follow the kid that was bragging home.

It was a beautiful afternoon and evening was approaching by the time the kid and his crew got to their street. Izzy followed them but the group of kids stopped in the middle of the street and was hanging out. Izzy took his gun out of his gym bag; he put his hoodie on and put the gun in the pouch on the front of the hoodie. He left his bag on the corner of the block and headed towards the guys. Izzy was nervous, he pulled his gun on people before to rob them but he hadn't shot the gun before let alone killed somebody. In his mind, he was going to pull out the gun and make the boy take him to Bear and kill Bear. As he approached the group of kids, they noticed him and before he could ever get his gun out the boys started beating him and kicking him. Izzy panicked and just took the beating balled in the fetal position covering his head with his hands. He started thinking he needs to stop being scared and pull his gun out and just start shooting. As he built up the courage to reach for his gun, the kicks and the punches stopped. He heard a deep voice and he opened his eyes to see who it was and there he was, the man that killed his parents. Izzy began to see pictures of his mom that his grandmother had around the house and how beautiful she was and the stories about his mother that his grandmother told him. He started thinking of the yearbook pictures he has seen of his mother and father. The prom pictures and he began to feel that fire and hatred again. Izzy was in a trance, he didn't hear any of the conversations that Bear and the boys were having. He just felt the pain, anger, and rage. His thoughts were interrupted when Bear reached his hand out to him. Izzy knew it was his chance, he couldn't punk out now, he thought. He reached out to Bear with his right hand but reached in his hoodie with his left hand. Izzy raised and pointed the gun at Bear simultaneously as Bear pulled him upright. Izzy pulled the trigger and a hole formed in Bear's forehead, blood began to run out, Bear's eyes rolled to his head, which dropped to the side and his body began to fall over.

The group of boys began running and screaming, Izzy didn't care about them, he couldn't take his eyes off of Bear. Izzy began to cry, tears running down his face. It was like it was all happening in slow motion. He couldn't make out the sounds around him but he could feel himself breathing heavily. He looked down at the body of Bear and began firing more shots into him until the clip was emptied. The gun not being able to shoot any more bullets snapped him out of his rage trance and he ran away looking back at the body one more time. People were sort of ducking but staring at him, he just ran as fast as he could, grabbed his gym bag and ran home. He ran into the house to his grandmother who was on her couch. She saw something was wrong, Izzy dropped the gun at the door, he was crying and he went and hugged his grandmother. She began to cry, Izzy said, "grandmother, I killed him, I killed the dude who killed my mama and daddy." The grandmother and Izzy didn't say another word. She just held her only grandbaby and they cried together. She started praying to God and calling out her decease daughter's name, Tia, repeatedly. She began rocking and squeezing Izzy as tight as she could as the police sirens grew louder and closer to her home. The police burst through the door, "Get the fuck on the ground."

THE END

www.ingramcontent.com/pod-product-compliance
Lightning Source LLC
Chambersburg PA
CBHW061525020726
47502CB00006B/2235